Tina Leonard

Last's Temptation

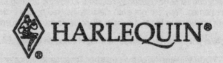

HARLEQUIN®

TORONTO • NEW YORK • LONDON
AMSTERDAM • PARIS • SYDNEY • HAMBURG
STOCKHOLM • ATHENS • TOKYO • MILAN • MADRID
PRAGUE • WARSAW • BUDAPEST • AUCKLAND

ISBN 0-373-75111-7

LAST'S TEMPTATION

Copyright © 2005 by Tina Leonard.

www.eHarlequin.com

Printed in U.S.A.

Books by Tina Leonard

HARLEQUIN AMERICAN ROMANCE

*Cowboys by the Dozen

Heather Tipton and Lorie Hart, for always being there. Joanne Reeson, you are a doll. Georgia Haynes, thank you for everything. Latesha Ballard, for making me smile. Fatin, your voice always cheers me. To all the Scandalous Ladies and Gal Pals, you are the best and truest friends.

Kimmie Eickholz, you are my best friend—
I love my sissy and her angels.

Isabel Sites, you're an awesome granny even if you are a feisty heroine.

Lisa and Dean, thank you for the Boy Scouts, lacrosse, drama, weird music and hair obsessions. I will always remember writing this book during your gall bladder removal, Dean. You were twelve, and having you at home for those three stolen weeks was an adventure that made the Jefferson boys stronger.

Many thanks to Stacy Boyd, whose memory is better than mine, and all the able editors and other people at Harlequin who have had a hand in making this series so much fun.

And to all the readers who have written to talk about it—it's been a dream come true.

Prologue

Dear sons,
You're growing up to be good men, and
your mother would be proud. I know I am.
Remember the things I've taught you. I hope
you can forgive me, but if I stay any longer on
the ranch where I see and hear your mother
every day, I'm going to die of a broken heart.
Always remember that I love you.
—Maverick Jefferson

Last Jefferson had been to hell and back.

He was not afraid of physical pain. Emotional
pain he preferred to avoid, as did all his brothers.
They claimed they were running from commitment, but the simple fact was that the men from
the Malfunction Junction ranch were die-hard

emotional-pain-avoidance junkies. No pain, all gain.

Last lived the motto as uncompromisingly as his eleven brothers. Being the youngest of twelve, he had watched. Learned. Now he possessed the soul of an escape artist. He loved his daughter, Annette. He loved his brothers and treasured his memories of growing up. And he had a soft spot for the mother of his daughter.

But, he thought, as he looked down at the California ground way, way below him, sometimes the only way to forget the past was to take a big flying leap into the future.

He held his breath the way he did before he rode a bull out of the chute. But this time instead of a bull carrying him hell-bent-for-leather into an arena, he ran until there was no ground left below his feet and nothing but a hang-glider canopy above him to keep him from leaving God's green earth altogether.

Chapter One

If it wasn't for the very shapely woman standing at the bottom of the California cliff, Last Jefferson might not have miscued his hang-glider landing, ending up in three feet of ocean instead of on the beach as he'd planned.

Last appreciated the female form, as did all of his brothers. Hers, he thought as she walked toward him, was worth the ocean water bath.

Until he saw the little boy and girl beside her.

Had he realized from his airborne position that the beautiful lady had two young children with her, he might have stayed dry. Unfortunately he'd been mainly focused on her sinuous shape and on the lovely cleavage gleaming above her bikini top.

The water was warmish, at least. He pulled off his helmet, grimacing.

"Are you all right?" the little boy asked. "You made a big splash when you hit the water."

"A *big* splash," his sister confirmed. "I bet the sea lions on their rocks heard it."

Last dragged himself out of the water, checking his canopy to make certain it was still in good shape. "You two remind me of my niece and nephew back home. And they're nothing but trouble," he said wryly. "You two run on back to your mom. I'm fine." *And I don't need any more wisenheimer children in my life.*

Nor did he need a woman. He'd had enough trouble with the female gender. He should have saved himself the crash landing. He was on a mind-clearing sabbatical here in California, and he'd learned the hard way that one-night stands were not mind-clearing exercises.

His toddler daughter was proof of that.

The shapely brunette finally caught up with her children. "Are you all right?" she asked him.

His mouth watered as he got a closer look at her face. "Yes. Thank you." Okay, God must have let one of his angels drop from the sky, because this woman was stunning.

Maybe she was a model. Wasn't California full of models and actresses?

"Can I help you?" she asked.

"Only by staying away," he said bluntly, although he appreciated her sun-browned waist above a long black sarong. Beneath the crepe fabric he could see very shapely legs. Orange-painted toenails peeped from her leather thongs. "I'm a loner."

"We're loners, too," the young boy said. "My mom's a magician."

Great. Just what he needed—someone who excelled in disappearing acts.

The Jefferson clan already possessed more disappearing acts than they needed, from their missing father Maverick to their eldest brother Mason, who had a habit of running off when he didn't want to deal with his feelings for a certain lady. Right now Last was focused on his own dis-appearing act, while his brother Crockett tried to make a family with his new wife, Valentine—who just happened to be Last's former one-night stand and the mother of Last's daughter, Annette. Privacy had seemed like the proper thing for Last to give the new family, and he'd chosen not to hang around like a disgruntled shadow.

No matter how pretty this young mother was, he wouldn't hang around here, either. "Goodbye," he said, hauling his hang-glider down the beach.

"Hey," the boy said, running after him. "My mom can pull a quarter from your ear."

"Look," Last said, not wanting to be mean, "I'll pull a ten-dollar bill from yours if you scram."

"Really?" The boy beamed while his sister looked on with doubt.

"Sure." Last took a ten from the elastic-covered hidden pocket of his long swim trunks, folded it, then handed it to the boy.

"Hey! That wasn't my ear!"

"But it is a ten. Now scram."

"I beg your pardon!" The gorgeous-vixen mother with dark hair and snapping blue eyes snatched the money from her son and handed it back to Last.

It *had* been in poor taste. Last opened his mouth to apologize, except the woman whirled around, dragging her kids, one in each hand, away before he could speak.

Hellfire. He shouldn't care, should he? He'd wanted them to bug off, and that's what they were doing. But he hadn't meant to hurt anyone's feelings.

"Jeez," he said under his breath, situating his canopy carefully on the sand. He ran after the brunette, noting that her rear view was as eye-pleasing as her front view.

Which meant spoon-style lovemaking would be a very pleasant option.

Whoa, he said to his unruly thoughts. With determination, he took his eyes off the swaying black sarong. "Excuse me."

She didn't turn around.

He jogged in front of her, holding up his palms in surrender. "Look, I'm sorry," he said.

"A sorry excuse for a gentleman," she snapped, passing him.

Gentleman? No one had ever accused him of being that. Gamely, he hustled past her. "My name's Last Jefferson. From Texas."

She marched past him.

The boy turned huge eyes toward him as the family walked away. "That's a weird name," he told Last. "Sort of like my mother's stage name."

Last trotted after the child, figuring he was the more receptive target for an apology. "What's your mother's stage name?"

"Poppy Peabody."

"Poppy Peabody?" That *was* a stage name.

"The hottest female magician performing today," the little girl said proudly. "Get your popcorn, take your seats, fellas—"

Poppy grimaced, tugging the children up the beach faster.

The "hot" part they had right. Last kept jogging alongside the boy, recognizing that the stubborn set of Poppy's shoulders meant he wasn't getting anywhere with her. "So what's your name?" he asked the boy.

"Curtis. My sister's name is Amelia."

"Nice names."

"Thanks. Is Last your stage name?"

"No." Last wished Poppy would slow down. Her legs were nearly as long as his and obviously far more used to sand power-walking. "It's all mine. Does your mother have a real name?"

"She's not really my mother," Curtis said in a confidential tone. "She's our aunt."

Aunt. Hmm. Last ignored the pleasure the knowledge gave him. "Name?"

Finally Poppy stopped. "Esmerelda Hastings," she said curtly. "I prefer Aunt Poppy to Aunt Esmerelda, and Poppy in general."

He blinked. "I can see where you might, although Esme is kind of cool, you have to admit. Not as dramatic, I guess."

"Poppy and Last," Amelia murmured, frowning. "That won't do. You're not The One."

"Amelia!" Poppy said. "I apologize," she told Last, her blush quite appealing. "They are home-schooled and quite precocious."

"I was homeschooled, for the most part," Last said. "We did go to public school for a few years, but more as a social exercise." Now that he had her attention, he refused to let it go. "Can we start over?" he asked with a smile.

"I suppose," she said reluctantly. "Although I try to discourage the children from talking to strangers. And certainly taking money from them is inappropriate."

"You speak just like Mary Poppins," Last said. "Very proper. Are you British?"

"Mary Poppins flew by parasol," Amelia interrupted. "And Mr. Last flew by hang-glider, though not very well," she finished thoughtfully. "It's *something* in common."

"I thought Mr. *Jefferson* did quite fine, except on the landing," Curtis said. "They probably have *lots* in common."

"Whew," Last said, "these two are certainly trying to set you up. I'm sorry I'm not available, if for no other reason than to see what they're up to."

Poppy smiled sadly. "My sister passed away a year ago, and it is the children's opinion that if they can marry me off, they will have a whole family. Like most children, having a whole family is their greatest wish."

"No father?" Last asked quietly, watching as the children were sidetracked by a bird flying overhead.

Poppy shook her head. "No one knows where he is."

"I know that routine," he said with a sigh.

"Sorry?" Poppy said.

Last hadn't seen his own father in years, though Mason kept up a diligent search. But Last wasn't ready to go into that, not here and not with a woman as pretty as Poppy/Esmerelda. "Hey, let's have lunch," he said instead. "I want to hear more about this magician's life you lead. Wasn't it 'the hottest female magician performing today'?"

Poppy blushed. "The children hear that every night from the announcer. Pay no attention to it."

"How can I not?" He grinned at the kids as they turned their gazes back to him. "It's true—at least the hot part. Now, magic, I don't believe in."

The children gasped. Poppy looked horrified.

"How do you think Mary Poppins flew?" Amelia demanded.

"Ropes and pulleys?" Last asked.

They all stared. *Must be British*, Last thought.

"Don't you believe in firefly magic and baby turtles that run to the sea without ever knowing what the sea is?" Curtis demanded.

"Instinct," Last said. "It's all instinct, a very good thing to have." Right now his was telling him that if he was smart, he'd be doing the cowboy-bachelor crawl away from this bunch.

Poppy drew herself up tall, which stretched her torso and raised her bikini top a bit, his practiced masculine eye noted. She had wonderfully taut skin, golden and plump with vitality.

"Magic is *everything*," Poppy said. "It moves the world. It heightens your senses. It's at the heart of your most fabulous moments."

"Nope. Those happen when I'm drinking a cold beer, and there's nothing magic about that except how fast I can make it disappear." He grinned, pleased by his own humor.

"Mr. Jefferson!" Poppy said.

"Oops. Another lapse. I *am* sorry." He gave her a crooked smile. "Neither I nor my eleven brothers are known for being role models."

Poppy sniffed. "I'll keep that in mind. Were you ever a child, Mr. Jefferson?"

"Most of my adult life," he said cheerfully.

"Although having a young daughter has certainly matured me."

"I doubt the veracity of that," Poppy said, "but I'll have to take your word for it. If you'll excuse us, we must decline your offer of luncheon. We have studies before tonight's show."

With the thought that he might not see Poppy again, he was suddenly in the mood to take in a show. What could it hurt? "Where will you be performing?"

"Goodbye," she told him, walking away.

"Damn," he said. "I'm not as smooth as I used to be."

From the way she'd said it, he knew better than to follow her. But for some reason he followed her anyway.

POPPY WALKED AWAY FROM the handsome stranger wishing her charges were just a bit less in shopping-for-a-father mode. It wasn't going to work. She had no desire for a permanent man, due to her lifestyle, and the children had no idea that marriage wasn't always filled with glittery magic.

It was hard work, and right now her efforts needed to be focused on the children. Amelia was ten, Curtis eight, and there would be many changes in their lives in the teen years. She had to think only of them, and a man would make things in her once-free life even more complicated. Five months ago, she'd been a happily traveling gypsy with no greater care than daily performances. She liked the bohemian lifestyle. But she'd had to settle down a bit since she'd inherited the children. That kind of focus was hard enough without the further distraction of a man.

The children didn't understand this. Amelia and Curtis only wanted a family, and were she in their circumstance, Poppy probably would have reacted the same way. But even if she was looking for marriage, the right man did not simply drop from the sky. Hunting for The One took effort and kissing lots of frogs.

She had an aversion to smooching frogs.

"You two must stop," she said now to Amelia and Curtis. "Please try to be satisfied that, for now, *we* are a family. And a good one. We're making it, aren't we?" she asked, bending down to look in their faces.

They nodded slowly, not convinced.

"The judge said it would be better if we were placed in a two-parent home," Amelia reminded her. "He said he'd examine our progress in a month."

"He doesn't like the fact that we travel with you in a circus," Curtis said, his blue eyes round. "He said it wasn't stable."

"True," Poppy agreed. "It's something to consider."

The judge certainly had been put off by her stage name and gypsy lifestyle. His suggested alternative was that the children live with Poppy's parents. Though they were far past the age of wanting to be responsible for children, the judge knew her parents personally and felt more comfortable with the stability he thought they would give the children.

It would be better for everyone if she could find a way to settle down, Poppy knew. And she was trying. "I will try harder," she said slowly. "I guess I could give marriage some consideration. But not to that man," she said quickly, dimming their suddenly hopeful faces. "He's just not for me."

They nodded, accepting her reason.

"We like living with you, Aunt Poppy," Amelia said. "We just want to stay with you."

"Maybe I should give up the land of make-believe and take a job as a teacher. It might impress the judge."

Surely it would. A sense of permanence was

what he'd seen lacking in her résumé. The only reason she'd been temporarily awarded custody of the children was that she was the only family member who'd come forward at the time of her sister's death to claim them. Frankly she felt her family's matters were none of the court's business, but in order to adopt the children, she'd had to file for custody.

The judge had taken exception to her, preferring, he'd said, the security of her parents' home. Or for Curtis and Amelia's father to reappear.

Old goat, Poppy thought angrily. "What does he know about me anyway?" she said. "I've been in the same job for ten years. I have a master's degree in English and a minor in business. A degree and job stability should speak favorably for me."

"It was the magic," Curtis said. "I think it bothered him."

Certainly it had bothered Mr. Jefferson. She had seen him visibly step back from her. If she was a teacher maybe none of this would be a problem. She'd have the children as hers. They would be a family.

"Excuse me," Last said, making his presence known and looking better than any man should in those long swim trunks and nothing else. "Before

I head off to my next adventure, I couldn't help but overhear… I think I could help you out."

"No, we don't want help from you," Poppy said, thinking of the children's marriage schemes. "You're too much like me. Unstable."

"I'm not unstable," Last said cheerfully, "but I will admit to being churlish, immature at times and living like the old cliché of the bachelor male."

"Which cliché would that be?" Poppy asked.

"Bitter and distrusting of women. Due to the fact that I was romanced and then sued by one. It's all fine now, but I'm holding on to the bitter and distrusting part as a cautionary reminder of what a female can do to a man. Sort of a souvenir."

Poppy couldn't help but laugh. "Goodbye, Mr. Bitter and Distrusting. We appreciate your offer of help, but you're a stranger and we have to think about our future."

"They seem to have a wedding in mind," he said, nodding toward the children, "but I'm really not the marrying kind."

"I didn't ask you," she said, annoyed.

"And except for my oldest brother Mason, I'm out of single brothers, so I can't even play matchmaker for you."

"Not necessary," Poppy snapped.

"But it's clear you're in a bind," Last continued, "and I've always been partial to coming to the rescue."

Poppy gasped. "I do not need rescuing!"

He winked. "Clearly you are on the railroad tracks of instability, ma'am, in the path of an oncoming judge-driven train. Here I am to save the day!"

"How do you propose to do that?" Poppy asked.

"You could go live on my ranch in Texas," Last said. "The mother of my child has vacated the house she was using. She's now living in town with my brother, Crockett. The house is empty, waiting for a happy family. Think about it," he said, "a Texas ranch, a job in town—it's the very image of stability."

Curtis's and Amelia's eyes glowed.

"It's not matrimony, but it would be a form of security. Mason is about to get roped into running for sheriff, I believe, by his dearest friend and enemy, Mimi." Last shook his head. "I don't know that Mason can worm out of Mimi's grasp on this one. Other than my brother Bandera, who lives in the house next door with his crew, and my brother Calhoun, who lives below the windmill with his, there's just horses, cows and sheep to liven up the days."

Poppy had to admit the picture was a tempting one. "Cowboys," she murmured.

"Nobody would mind you living there. Olivia—Calhoun's wife—used to travel in a gig with her horse, Gypsy, and her father-in-law, who was a rodeo clown. Right up your alley, huh?"

Poppy hesitated. She wasn't sure anymore what was "up her alley." The children had changed her life. That was all she did know.

"What made you become a magician anyway?" he asked.

"My master's thesis was about beliefs. Ninety percent of people want to believe in something magical. Good fortune of some kind," she murmured. "I decided to test the theory."

"So you're in the circus because of your thesis?"

She looked at him thinking that he alone was enough to make a woman believe in good fortune. Strong-muscled and tall, the dip in the ocean had left his skin gleaming. She shivered. "I may pursue a doctorate one day. It's good to collect more data. Can I make people believe?" An unwilling smile touched her lips. "You're certainly a doubter."

"Yeah, but I'm hardheaded by nature. I don't want to believe in anything that I can't rope or ride."

Poppy nodded. "I understand. That's how the

majority of people sampled felt. Put, of course, in different terms than yours."

"But I'm always up for an adventure," he added with a devilish grin. "And that's what I'm offering to you, Professor."

She looked into his chocolate-brown eyes. "I don't even know you."

He grinned. "But don't you feel the magic?"

Curtis and Amelia looked up at her. "Do you?" Curtis asked.

"Aunt Poppy?" Amelia said.

Goose pimples raised on her arms. "Children, it's time to go. The sun is setting, and that means a bit of a chill this time of year. Goodbye, Mr. Jefferson. Good luck to you on your adventures."

She escaped, her heart pounding. Oh, she *had* felt the magic.

It was the one thing she never wanted to feel again.

Chapter Two

"It's okay to be a fake," Poppy said under her breath as she and the children walked up a small set of steps to get to her car.

She didn't believe in real magic any more than Last Jefferson did. She only believed in the kind she could produce under the big top, wearing a foxy bikini, a skirt with sequins and some fishnets.

The children should never know. They clung to her stories of magic, believing in fairy princesses and air-hung castles and all good things that could be found if one just wished for them.

"I could be wrong," she said, "but it seems appropriate to encourage imagination and creativity in you two. What else are myths, fairy tales and legends for?"

Curtis and Amelia looked up at her, their dear

faces round and sweet. Poppy just wanted Curtis and Amelia to have the joy of being children.

Drat the cowboy for making her wonder if reality would be better for them. *Esme indeed.*

"I am certain Mr. Jefferson just recited some cowboy tall tales to us," she said. "Perhaps he doesn't even live on a ranch. Why would a true cowboy want to fly off a cliff?"

Amelia's eyes widened. "The same reason someone wants to walk on the moon?"

Poppy shook her head. "I do believe the gentleman was yanking our chains. Let's forget about him."

"I've never met a real cowboy before," Curtis said. "I wonder if he has a holster."

"Oh." Poppy crossed the street, protectively watching for traffic. "Westerns are not reality."

"But when John Wayne—"

"We *know*," Amelia said impatiently. "No more discussions about the genius of John Wayne, Curtis."

Poppy stopped when they were on the opposite corner of the street. She glanced down at her niece and nephew. "It may be time for you two to be enrolled in public school."

They looked at her.

"Why?" Curtis asked. Amelia stared silently.

"Because. We may have veered too far into

the land of make-believe. It's possible that the judge is right."

"You called him an old goat," Curtis reminded her.

She sighed, regretting the moment of her quick tongue filing its nervous complaint. "I did. But he may be right about the stability issue."

"Why?" Amelia asked. "You said stability was for people who accepted that adventure was dead. That fortune wasn't built nor determined by people who wouldn't take a chance."

"True, but I may be working on a new hypothesis. Children who are taught the realities of life do not end up flying from cliffs."

Their eyes went wide.

Poppy shrugged. "It's something to consider. And I must always consider your welfare, first and foremost." She squeezed their hands. "Kids, look. I have no experience as a mother. I don't even know what I'm doing. It's possible the judge has reason to be concerned about the way I'm raising you." What was so great about life under a big top or on a stage anyway?

It could be time to stop doing research. She'd made a lot of people believe in her magic. She'd proven to herself that people did want to believe, if only for the moment, and that taking their cares away for a while was a gift. Maybe that was the only magic she could really believe in. "And it could be that your mother wouldn't have wanted you to live such a bohemian lifestyle."

"Excuse me, for the last time," she heard from behind her. "I swear."

The cowboy had followed her and the children across the street. Bare-chested still. Her breath left her. If he was a stalker, he was a very handsome one.

"I need to clarify one thing," Last said. "Just in case you ever decide to take me up on my offer."

"I won't."

"I'm not planning on being around there much, at least for a while," he admitted.

She gazed at him.

"If I'm the reason you might not consider it, that is."

"I don't know that the judge would approve of us picking up and leaving the state at this time. Also, my parents really need me—or at least I tell myself they do."

Last nodded. "I understand. And to tell you the truth, while life on a ranch can be stable, we Jeffersons do *not* have a reputation for stability."

She put a hand on her hip. "I wouldn't have guessed."

"But the ranch is in a town populated by very nice characters. Again, something to consider, just in case you change your mind. It's the Jefferson ranch in Union Junction, Texas, better known as Malfunction Junction."

The kids grinned. Poppy did not. "The ranch, not the town, is better known as Malfunction Junction?"

"Specifically the nickname refers to my family," he said softly in a voice that sent silken shivers over Poppy's skin. "It's the bane of our existence. We are a malfunctioning crew, whether we admit it or not."

He was a rogue and a daredevil, she realized. Perhaps a bit crazy.

Everything she did not need in her life.

"We're late," she told the cowboy. "I hope to never see you again."

He looked hurt. She shook her head, turning to walk away. The kids peered over their shoulders at him.

"Oh, he looks like a puppy," Amelia observed. "Poor cowboy."

Poppy sighed.

"Why don't you like him, Aunt Poppy?" Curtis asked.

"I have to be very careful," she said, specifically

thinking about rogues and daredevils who made a woman do stupid things…bedroom things.

Last was a delicious specimen of male. No illusion of magic was required to make him more visually desirable than he was.

"Malfunction Junction sounds like fun," Amelia said.

"What we don't need is another circus in our lives," Poppy said firmly. "And that's exactly what it sounds like to me." After another moment of brisk walking, she asked quietly, "Is he still following?"

"No," Curtis said. "He turned around and walked away a few minutes ago."

"After waving goodbye," Amelia said. "You know how you always tell us not to talk to strangers?"

"Yes," Poppy said. "And now you see why."

There was no reply for a second.

"Well," Curtis said, "at least I finally met a real John Wayne."

"We don't know that," Poppy stated. "He wasn't wearing a hat or boots."

"I know that," Curtis said. "A real cowboy doesn't need his hat to be real."

"When the lion tamer offered to marry you, you said he was too wild," Amelia pointed out. "When the ringmaster offered, you said his hat was too tall and you weren't sure what was under there. The cowboy only offered us his ranch, and he won't even be there. Wouldn't that mean we can trust him?"

"I don't know," Poppy said with determination. "And I love you two too much to find out."

"Do you like any man, Aunt Poppy?" Curtis asked.

"Yes. I like *you*. Now forget about the cowboy, children, and let's think about tonight's performance."

But she knew why he stayed on their minds. Brave, daring, somehow vulnerable—he was a very appealing character to two young children who were growing up needing a fairy-tale hero. And to the woman learning to be their mother.

LAST JEFFERSON KNEW when he'd been given the winter-frozen shoulder. No meant no, and that little lady had just handed him a very firm *no*.

Too bad. The kids had been cute. Whistling, he went to pick up his hang-glider, trying to decide if he had enough daylight left for another go at his technique.

Or he could go attend this "show" the children had mentioned. Tickets were public, weren't they? And he could just look up the location on the

Internet. Poppy would never know. He wouldn't mind seeing a bit of this "magic" hocus-pocus they'd talked about.

Then again, why did he care? He'd gotten himself in enough trouble once, a long time ago, by drinking a bottle of a supposedly mystical potion. "Surely I've learned from my mistakes. Mystical things are bad for me."

He *should* know better. He didn't need a woman, no matter how alluring. His daughter didn't need one more person introduced into her life in a parental role; right now assimilating her new family of Crockett and Valentine would be challenge enough.

He needed to think with his mind and not his heart—or that more traitorous region of his body.

More time in the air hanging from something should clear his mind.

And yet, he would love to make Esme change that formal, snippy tone she'd used when she'd said, "Mr. Jefferson," to a gasping, grateful, *Oh, Mr. Jefferson!*

He couldn't afford to indulge the fantasy.

"One more go?" asked the hang-glider attendant.

"I think not," Last said. "Thanks, though."

After changing into jeans and a shirt, he got

into his truck. Two weeks driving the scenic route in north California, then heading to Africa for bungee jumping had felt like the right decision when he'd left Texas. The trip had been the perfect excuse for giving his brother and his new wife some family time.

No one knew, but it was really hard on Last to think about the new little family, no matter how much he loved Crockett. He wanted to be Annette's only father, even if he knew that wasn't possible. Damn lucky he was that her stepfather would be Crockett.

Still, it stung. His lips drew into a tight line, his gaze catching sight of brightly colored red tents as he drove only a few miles up the road. The tents could signify only one thing: the circus was in town and very near. He'd bet this was Esme's gig.

He couldn't resist.

In fact, he wouldn't even try, he decided, parking his truck on the grounds and buying a ticket. Sneaking into the big top, he noted that his seat was far up and away from where Poppy or the children might spy him. The elderly gentleman seated beside him seemed harmless and likely to mind his own business, so Last was satisfied.

Checking his ticket stub, he realized he had

about an hour to wait. He began dozing under his hat, somewhat bored by the lack of bulls and bucking broncs.

"The hottest magician on planet Earth," he heard the announcer yell, making him sit straight up. "Poppy Peabody!"

Last's jaw dropped as Esme rode into the arena on the back of a white pony, wearing a bikini-type garment so sexy he could only call it delightful.

No wonder the judge was having a bit of trouble seeing Poppy as a role model and a good guardian. Last grinned. The elderly gentleman next to him looked as though he'd never seen a showgirl of any kind and might have a coronary.

Esme was adorable, with black strands of cloth hanging from the bikini bottom and a feathery black sequined headdress pluming from her long ebony hair. Something jumped in his jeans, and Last realized he was more attracted to her than he'd been to anyone in his life—well worth the ticket price he'd paid to get in.

He realized the flip-flopping children in the act were Amelia and Curtis. They flipped onto the small stage where Esme dismounted, and as music filtered through the arena she put Curtis into a box, concealing him.

A moment later she was sawing through him. Last's heart thundered. The judge was right! The children were young and impressionable and probably easily scared! Last leaned forward, knowing in his heart that Esme wouldn't hurt them. They'd probably done this act a hundred times—but still, he was relieved when Curtis reappeared with no blood spurting from his "halved" body.

Then Last's heart went completely still as Amelia was raised on a pulley, seemingly as if by magic wings, to the ceiling. Esme approached the center of the stage, instructing Amelia to fly. And fly she did, nearly to Last's seat. Maybe she'd seen him! It seemed as if they'd made eye contact. Last wasn't certain. As she swung back, to the gasps of the audience, Esme yelled, "Disappear!" and she did! Last craned his neck looking for Amelia, but she was gone. Poof!

He was very angry with Poppy Peabody.

She had certainly made a believer out of him. His entire collar was soaked with perspiration.

A second later the vein in his temple went back to normal when Curtis and Amelia stood beside their aunt, to the delighted applause of the audience. Annoyed at himself for falling for grandiose tricks and a woman in a spectacularly pleasing costume, he stomped down the stairs, preparing to exit and hit the road.

But he was stopped by a man in a very tall hat.

"You are the cowboy?" the man asked.

"I suppose," Last replied. "Some days more than others."

"Come with me."

"I don't think so," Last said. "I paid my ticket, and that means I leave when I want."

"Poppy wants you," the man in the ringmaster's costume insisted.

"Poppy?" The hottest magician on the planet—or in California or whatever—wanted him? Last blinked. "All right, stranger. Move along. I'm right behind you."

He walked into a makeup room where Esme stood surrounded by her charges, a lion tamer, a man in a gorilla costume and the ringmaster.

"Mr. Jefferson!" Curtis and Amelia cried.

"I told you he was here, Aunt Poppy," Amelia said.

Last crossed his arms. "Nice show," he said, meaning *costume,* though now was not the time to say it. The atmosphere in the room was distinctly testosterone-charged.

"Thanks." Poppy turned to her friends. "I thank you for your offers of marriage, all of you. However, this is the man who would like to take me to his ranch and this is the man I have chosen."

Last stood still, not even allowing himself to blink. What was she saying? He couldn't marry her. He couldn't marry anyone, but especially not someone who was as unstable as he was. Together they'd be combustible!

The ringmaster nodded. "Come," he told Last.

"I prefer to stay here," Last said.

The gentleman seemed to take exception to that, so Last shrugged and followed the guy in the too-tall hat. "Great duds," he said.

"You can do better?" the man asked in his heavily accented voice.

Last figured by the pleading look in Curtis's and Amelia's eyes that he'd better follow along. "Welcome to the family," the ringmaster said, opening a curtain to reveal the innermost workings of the circus.

It was far busier and more colorful than anything he'd ever seen at a rodeo. "Wow. Crazy."

The ringmaster nodded. "You are sure you want to take our Poppy to Texas with you?"

"Uh—"

Amelia and Curtis nodded emphatically. Last recognized desperation when he saw it.

"The judge was sitting right next to you, Mr. Last," Curtis said. "We think he wasn't very happy."

So reassurance of stability was in order. Surprisingly, he was eager to do the reassuring. "Yes. Absolutely. I'll take Esme—I mean *Poppy* and company to Texas."

Everyone stopped when the ringmaster gestured. "This is Poppy's husband-to-be," he announced, and everyone applauded. Sweat broke out on Last's forehead under his hat.

He'd offered the ranch, not a ring! Mason had nearly blown a gasket when a pregnant Valentine had shown up a while back. But Mason was going to *kill* him if Last brought home a ready-made family.

"THAT WAS AWKWARD," Poppy said once the three of them were packed into his truck. "I apologize."

Last seemed too stunned to reply. She could tell he was feeling a mixture of anger and annoyance. "Last?"

"You look better without the stage makeup," he said. "Though I really dug the costume."

She blinked. "I always thought the plumes were a bit over-the-top."

"No way. Made you look like a fan dancer."

Then he went back to staring at the road.

"You can drop us off at the ranch you'd mentioned," Poppy said, feeling sick at how she'd used him. The judge had been adamant tonight about taking the children and…she'd had no choice. "I don't really expect you to marry me."

"I should hope not," Last said. "I can't marry anyone. Ever. It's a conscience thing."

"I understand. And I don't want to get married. It just got very heated back there. The lion tamer said the judge was a bit upset, and the ringmaster said I needed to make a magical disappearance but in a way in which they could responsibly cover my leaving. You provided the perfect cover."

Last sighed. "How?"

"They told him we were leaving on a honeymoon. And then you were taking us to your Texas ranch to see how we liked living life in one place, in the country, far from all the glitter."

"I see. Did he buy it?"

She shrugged. "Enough to give us some time. We have to be back in a month, of course, so he can check on the children's well-being before he'll give me final custody."

Last felt sorry for Esme and her kids. It was

tough being in the middle of a custody battle—he knew that too well—and there was no reason for him to say that everything would work out. It might not.

"Well, you'll like the ranch," he said. "Everyone around there is certifiable but nice. You'll fit in just fine. The kids can go to school—"

Clapping erupted from the backseat. Esme turned around. "I'm surprised at you two!"

"It sounds like fun!" Amelia said.

"Yeah," Curtis said. "I'm going to be just like Mr. Last. A cowboy!"

Last sighed. "You're going to get me in big trouble with your aunt." Frowning, he said, "Hey, since you're not in the circus anymore, can I call you Esme instead of your stage name?"

She blinked. "I've never gotten used to Esmerelda. I was teased in school over it, and when the ringmaster named me Poppy Peabody, I was so relieved."

"I know exactly how that feels," Last said. "Imagine your name being Last. And being last in a long line of brothers. Never mind the name games. Fast Last, Lasting Gas and so on. I pounded on some kids in my youth."

"I didn't," Esme said. "I pretended I didn't hear them. Esmerelda Smells was the main nickname."

"Oh. Bummer." He brightened. "You smell wonderful to me."

She looked at him askance. "Thank you. When were you close enough to tell?"

"I can tell." He nodded. "Women come in all flavors under the sun, and I love them every one."

She stared at him.

"Sorry." Last looked only a tiny bit ashamed. "Well, I do."

She narrowed her eyes at this too-playful cowboy. "I have the strangest feeling you didn't bear the heaviest load at the ranch," Poppy said. "You're far too relaxed."

"Mason bore most of the burden," Last admitted cheerfully. "And I was ever the baby wearing rose-colored glasses. My brothers all had problems. Tex, for example, had *budus interruptus*."

"Sounds painful."

"It was. For all of us. He was a madman when things didn't go his way with his plants. No different than the rest of us, of course. Everybody's got hang-ups. Probably even you."

She looked out the opposite window.

"You can share if you like," he said. "I'm listening."

She checked over her shoulder. Amelia and Curtis had fallen asleep, their heads resting against each other's.

"I never wanted to be tied down," she said quietly. "I was the girl who never dreamed of The Prince. The One. I was always hanging around my grandparents, learning card tricks. Sleight of hand. Even ventriloquism."

"Great," Last said. "A woman who's more into freedom than me. It's almost like meeting my mirror image, only more frightening because you're hot as hell."

"Really?"

He nodded. "Definitely. That's why once I drop you at the ranch I've got to go. I've already had one night of passion go wrong on me. I have no intention of repeating history."

"Did you love her?"

"We don't even remember the night very much," Last admitted. "But the aftermath was a killer, never mind the hangover. My baby is an angel, though. She's gonna be a man slayer when she grows up. Looks like her mom, thank heaven, except with a bit of darkness in her hair and eyes." He glanced over at her. "Sort of like you."

Poppy felt something tingle down her spine,

something very much like a magic trick played perfectly.

"The problem is," he said with a wicked gleam in his eyes, "I would love to make love to you. But I just can't afford that mistake again."

"That scared?"

"I told you, I'm living the cliché," he said, grinning at her with a wink. "The ultimate untamable bad boy. All I can say is that you would like it. I would like it. And it would definitely be something we both remembered."

That tingle turned into a warning shiver. She was not at a place in her life where she could be seduced. Even by such a master of seduction as this cowboy, who, no doubt, was not exaggerating his skills. "Maybe I should have accepted the lion tamer," she murmured.

"They broke the mold for sure when they made him," Last said. "Why didn't you marry him?"

"I knew he was asking me as a friend. I didn't want that, even for the sake of the children. It wasn't fair to him."

"And the ringmaster? I got the sense that he was rather fatherly."

She nodded. "He was. He offered, but I saved him from his kindness. Staying with them, with the circus, wouldn't have endeared me to the judge. It was time to go."

"And along I came," Last said, turning off the highway onto a side road. "I want one last drive along the beach before heading back toward the land of stability." He gave a heavy sigh. "I must warn you, we have a strong dose of superstition in our family. And if I get the sense even for a second that you might be invoking The Curse in me, I might have to…to send you into town to live with the Union Junction stylists. You'd like them," he said. "They'd mother your kids to death. And the children would be closer to school."

"What curse?" Poppy asked. "I don't usually believe in such things."

"Good," Last said, satisfied. "This one has to do with love, and it's happened to every single one of my brothers. When they found their true loves, they got hurt."

"That's…silly," Poppy said. "What have I gotten myself into?" She glanced into the backseat, where the children slept, comfortable in the double cab.

"I'm sure everything's going to be just fine," Last told her. He peered through the windshield. "What the hell is that beside the road?"

"A dog?" Poppy looked harder. "A sea lion!"

"No way," Last said. "They're too fat to get all the way over here." They were close enough to the ocean to see the waves from the road, but the road was still too far for a sea lion, at least by Last's standards. Stopping the truck, he said, "I'm going to go check on whatever it is."

Poppy watched anxiously as he snuck up on the hapless creature. She turned on the truck's hazard lights so drivers coming around the narrow, winding road would see them.

To her surprise, she saw Last struggling with the animal. It seemed as if he was trying to push it back toward the sea. And just when it appeared he might be winning, the animal turned on him. Flippers and arms battled. Gasping, Poppy hit the horn with all her might. Startled, the animal lumbered back toward the ocean. Last lay on the ground for a moment before picking himself up and dragging himself into the seat of his truck. "Just like the rodeo," he said. "I'm always getting tossed."

"Are you all right?" Poppy asked. "That was horrible!"

"I'm fine," Last said. "By golly, it was harder to corral than a bull. It nearly got the best of me!"

"That's because it *was* a bull, obviously," Poppy said. "A junior sea lion bull, beached and confused."

"Yes. And damned unappreciative." Last checked his ripped shirt. "It took exception to me saving it."

"It didn't look like you were saving it. It wanted to kill you! What made you try to move a wild creature?"

He groaned. "I move all kinds of wild creatures all the time, some that weigh a couple tons and have impressive horns and sharp hooves. Believe me, I didn't think it would be any more difficult than throwing a cow to the ground or corralling a mad bull. It looked like a bunch of harmless blubber lying there all pathetic."

"You smell like seal," Poppy said. "You're lucky to be alive."

"I'm just badly hurt," Last said with a groan. "I may need a doctor."

"Scoot over. I'll drive you to the hospital." As she stared at him clutching his side, she shook her head. "I want you to know this one doesn't count."

He looked at her through pained eyes. "What one?"

"The Curse thing. The don't-hurt-me thing."

The pain left Last and he sat up, staring at her. "Oh, no," he said, his tone angry. "Oh, no, no, *no*. You *cannot* be The One."

Chapter Three

Last had known this woman and her children were trouble the moment he'd laid eyes on them. They were even more trouble now that they were going to cost him an airplane ticket out of California and into the land of ultimate bungee jumping. Most particularly, they were going to get him in a lot of trouble with Mason, who already thought Last hadn't properly learned the Condom Song since he'd become an unwed father. Bringing home two more children would only make matters more awkward between him and his eldest brother.

Last stared at Poppy for a few moments, his whole body screaming with pain and his mind shouting horrific echoes of denial.

"This time, The Curse is wrong. Actually, I feel fine now." He struggled to sit up in the driver's seat. "I'm completely healthy, with not one pain an aspirin can't fix. I just need you to drive."

"What?" Esme asked.

He took a deep, shaken breath. If he was honest, he'd admit the sea lion had scared the hell out of him. What looked like harmless, soft flubber had really been equal to any mad thing he'd met on the ranch, including Mason. There was a possibility he had a cracked rib.

"You drive," Last repeated, getting out of the truck to limp around to the passenger side. "I'm according you the honor of driving a man's truck, which has never been driven by a female."

She shook her head. "No way. I want no part of you or your truck." She sniffed in a hoity-toity way, but he didn't have the strength to argue with her.

"Look. Get your foxy little ass out of my seat so I can sit down."

"You're hurt!"

"No, I'm not," he said through gritted teeth.

"I think you are."

"I think I'd know if I was!" A star passed before his vision that seemed as big as Halley's Comet. He slumped into the seat she'd vacated. *"Drive."*

She cleared her throat. "Last, can I say something?"

"Sure, magician."

"I need to stop by and say goodbye to my parents. Plus the kids and I need to pack a suitcase. And I really would love to get out of my costume."

The galaxy was threatening to take him over. "Do whatever you have to," he said. "Just don't ever tell a soul that a rubbery seal nearly got the best of me."

"It'll be our secret." She pulled out onto the road, winding back toward the highway. "I could make a pit stop at the hospital—"

"I am not hurt," he insisted. "I probably just caught a bit of wind shear when I was hang-gliding and didn't realize I'd reorganized my internal organs at that time. Next breeze I'll be fine."

Her giggle was annoying. "Whatever."

He kept his eyes tightly shut, enjoying Esme's smooth driving. Okay, he would let her drive all the way to the ranch. There he could find some tape to bandage his rib. Shoot, he'd been hurt worse than this in rodeos and had still dragged himself back to the ranch. He could do it again.

Only…this time there was Mason to think about. Now that would be pain that would send him into the next galaxy. Cracking one eye open, he stared over at Esme as she concentrated on the road. Damn, she was pretty. So exotic. And good to her family. He liked that in a woman. And she had a little bit of attitude, which he thought spiced her up just fine.

His eye traveled from her top to the sequined band at her hips where the cloth strips hung. Her exposed waist was a smooth road, he decided poetically, one which he would certainly like to navigate. Such a shame she was totally wrong for him.

Valentine hadn't been right for him, and she was the mother of his child. So there was no way that Esme could be the one. With her two kids and her unstable ways she was the worst-case scenario of what could happen if a man didn't look before he leaped off the cliff of romance.

"You're staring at me," she said. "With one eye. And it gives you a remarkably Popeye-ish appearance."

"You could have said pirate," he complained.

"Your eye is pretty swollen. I feel Popeye is appropriate."

"Lovely. Popeye and Poppy sitting in a tree—"

"Oh, good grief." She stopped the truck. "I think you have a concussion."

"I swear I do not, madam. I am insulted you would suggest it."

He thought he heard her say, "What a fruitcake" under her breath. Magnanimously he ignored that.

"So what exactly does the judge think your parents could do better with the children than you do?" he asked.

She sighed, starting to drive again. "Send them to a regular school, give them a one-home environment, all the things children need. I know it's true, but he simply does not understand that I've been caring for my parents for some time. The strain of losing my sister was too much for them. Unless you've lost a child, I don't think you can understand that pain."

He nodded, thinking about his father. "Actually I do understand a little." Maverick had never gotten over losing his wife, and as much as Last hated the fact that his father had left them, at least Maverick hadn't let himself die from grief. Last could remember their father, his skin gray from shock, his gait changed—he shook his head. "The ranch is a great place. You're doing the right thing. If you think you can handle it."

"I do," she said. "Thank you for taking us with you."

He groaned, trying not to think about Mason and the coronary to come. "Don't mention it." But he couldn't help thinking about the children in the back of the truck. "I wasn't certain I liked you having them in your act," he admitted now.

Esme looked at him. "They're with me all the time. And I teach them, as did other people in the troupe. What was wrong with it?"

"I don't know. When you sawed Curtis—" he lowered his voice "—you scared me. It seemed almost medieval."

Stopping the car, she peered into his face. "Are you sure you didn't get a screw knocked out of you?"

"All my screws are tight," he replied airily, "but I really did not like it when you made Amelia disappear. That was much too high for a little girl. I was afraid she'd fall."

"She wears a harness that you can't see, and there's a cleverly concealed net below, in case something did go wrong."

"I knew you'd take all the proper precautions, but still I was afraid," he admitted. "I don't know how your circus act is scarier than teaching a child how to rodeo—and we all got busted up at one time or another—and yet it bothered me."

She blinked. "You sound like the judge."

He held up a hand. "I don't mean to. I'm just trying to figure out why it bothered me so much."

"Perhaps you believed in the magic," she suggested.

"No," he said. "I most certainly did not."

"What is the difference between my act and yours?" she demanded. "All this superstition nonsense?"

"That is a Jefferson fact," he insisted, "and you're simply using optical illusions."

She laughed at him as she pulled up in front of a small cottage-style bungalow. "Home," she said. "Do I need to help you out of the truck?"

"I'm fine." Stubbornly he crawled out of the passenger seat. "Though I wonder if your parents have a teeny-weeny bandage I could borrow."

"For your ribs?"

"Never mind." Her trouble was that she was so sure of herself. So pigheaded. And, unfortunately, so sexy.

He just had to stop thinking of her that way.

"Come inside," she said, tucking one of his arms over her shoulder. "My parents will fix you a cup of tea."

He needed some Jack Daniel's in that tea, but he refused to inquire as to her parents' preference for something harder than chamomile. Trying not to groan, he let Esme lead him inside the small house.

It smelled of cinnamon, he realized. Very much like Valentine's bakery. Suddenly he missed home—he missed his little daughter—and he dreadfully regretted all the actions that had brought him broken to this place in his life.

"Hello?" a kindly elderly woman said to him. "Are you hurt?"

He looked into the gentle blue eyes of a woman who had to be eighty years old. "I think so, ma'am. But I swear, your daughter had nothing to do with it."

She smiled. "I should think not. Come in and lie down next to Chester."

He hoped Chester was a very still, very plump pillow, but it turned out to be a large, old yellow dog on the sofa. Across from the sofa was a recliner, and an elderly gentleman raised an arm at Last.

"Don't mind Chester," he said. "He won't mind you."

Last wouldn't have minded a pig at this moment. Sinking onto the sofa, he laid his head back, gasping as he stared at the ceiling.

"Where did you find him, dear?" the mother asked the daughter. "Did he take over the lion tamer's position prematurely?"

"Not exactly," Esme replied. "Let me get the

children out of the truck and put them to bed. We may have to spend the night, Mom."

"Fine, fine. I have plenty of eggs for breakfast. Young man, do you like bacon?"

"His name is Last, Mom."

"Last?" She sounded confused, and Last was too tired to explain. "All right. Do you like bacon, Last?"

"I would really like an aspirin, ma'am," he said, before saying, *"Timber!"* and crashing face-first into the elderly dog's pillow.

"That's right, Chester, you take good care of him," Last heard Esme's father say before he finally gave up to the sleep that wanted to claim him. He had to. He'd fallen into the circus of hell, and clearly there would be no rescue or safety net for this cowboy.

ESME STARED DOWN at Last, not quite sure what to do with him. Her parents had gone to bed. The children were tucked in. Chester had given up the sofa to the flailing cowboy. She folded her arms, wondering why Last was so dead set against seeing a doctor. She was pretty certain he needed one, the big goon.

Bending down to get close to his face, she touched his forehead. "That's what you get for trying to save everything, you big silly."

He didn't move. Poppy studied his face, glad to be able to do it when he wasn't piercing her with those watchful eyes of his. "Maybe you have a record," she said, moving his hair away from his face. "That would be one reason you wouldn't want to be seen. Which would also make you bad for me. Worse than you already are."

A steel hand reached out, grabbing her wrist. "I have no record," Last said. "I am very good for you, and you should be grateful."

To her shock, he pulled her on top of him. She was so surprised she stared down at him, an inch from his face.

"Now let's see who's bad for whom," he said, kissing her deeply, his hands framing her face as he held her captive. Over and over he kissed her, his lips firm and demanding and so practiced that she gave herself over to the wonderful feeling of being kissed by this stranger who didn't wear fur or a too-tall hat. His hands sneaked down to her bottom, slipping into the pockets of the clam diggers she wore, holding her tightly against him.

"I think you're bad for me," he said. "I'm certain of it."

"I think you're worse," she told him, holding his face so that she could kiss him some more. Good heavens, a woman should be kissed like this at least once a week! It was more than magic; she felt sprinkles and stardust and all the accoutrements of the fairy-tale land she'd spoken of but never experienced.

"I may be worse, but your kisses make me feel better than an aspirin." He rolled her beneath him. "Make me feel even better."

He was making her feel more than she ever had, so Poppy complied, winding her arms around him as he lay full-length against her. There was hardness against her from top to bottom and something much more in the middle, making her eyes water from the pleasure of knowing that this man wanted her that way.

"We're bad for each other," he reminded her.

"I know," she replied.

"I like it," he said.

"I'm certain I do, too." She desperately wanted to pull his pants off and check out the rest of him, though his mouth was quite a wonderful place to start.

"I keep telling myself that I should have learned my lesson by now."

"Pfft," Poppy said. "You talk a big game, but I'm not listening."

"That's your problem." He sneaked a hand

inside her shirt, caressing her stomach. "I find your truculence annoying. And somehow stimulating."

"I find your cockiness disturbing. And somehow attractive."

"Aren't we a pair then?" Lazily he ran a hand to the small of her back.

She hummed in pleasure—until common sense tried to reassert itself. "Now that I think about it, how do I know you're even who you say you are? I should stay right here with my parents."

"You should," Last agreed. "But this is a very small house for two growing children. Your parents seem a bit tired to take on two grandchildren and a daughter who should have been out of the nest a *long* time ago." He clucked at her. "You would be a burden."

"You are an ass," she replied. "I give my parents money to live on. They are not burdened by me."

"Glad to hear that you're responsible." Last bit her neck, gently cupping her fanny at the same time. "Guess you just have to prove it to the judge."

"That's where you come in."

"And what do I get out of the matter?"

"Nothing," she said, "because you have hero tendencies. Saving small, blubbery things from being beached by life."

He pushed against her, making her quite aware of his desire for her. "I do not want to save you. I'm only taking you with me because of your children. I've always liked children. Twenty women came to our ranch one day and one of them—Annabelle—had a little baby. I saw that adorable baby and I knew right then and there that Malfunction Junction needed lots of children. And I was right. My job there is done, as my brothers have populated our ranch so that now even Christmases without our mother or our father are happy occasions."

"And you even have your own child."

"Yes," he said softly, "but she was a surprise. You and yours I have taken on willingly."

Her breath caught. "Why?"

"You said it yourself. Small, blubbery things," he said, nipping at her lips. "Helpless and cute."

"I am not helpless," Poppy said. "Only in poor circumstances."

"Still, you need me."

"You are a male chauvinist." She got off the sofa. "But a convincing kisser. You almost made me like you."

He laughed softly, his gaze unconvinced by her fib. "And you don't now?"

She crossed her arms. "No. I think you are delusional. By dawn's light, I will forget that you are a macho opportunist and give you a ride home."

"Give me a ride home?" His gaze watched her lazily.

"Yes. With your injuries, the only way you're getting home is by airplane or with someone driving you. Speaking of your condition, I do believe you are using passion to get your mind off your pain. In no way are you fit enough to drive yourself to Texas, you faker."

"So you're saying you're doing me a favor."

"Absolutely," she said stiffly. "And I'll thank you not to forget it."

"Yes, ma'am."

He put his cowboy hat back on, grinning at her. She hated his know-it-all attitude. And his sure sexiness. Pursing her lips, she left the room, her heart and mind racing with so many emotions she had never before experienced that she didn't know where to start to sort them out.

But she knew one thing for certain: she had to think of two little orphans before she thought of her own wayward heart. Curtis and Amelia were in a fragile, delicate situation. If the judge didn't feel that Poppy was suitable for caring for them, he would give those rights to her parents. As Last had noted, her parents were frail and elderly. Heaven forbid something should happen to them, but if it did, what would become of the children?

It would not do for her to become involved in a relationship now with a man who had no desire for his own family. He already had a complicated family and he had a phobia about acquiring more commitments in his life.

She actually understood his feelings. Before her sister's death, she had always thought she would follow her own guiltless path of exploration.

Now the idea of taking that path felt almost self-centered. She should have helped her sister more when Beryl was alive. After her husband had left, to disappear for good, Poppy had figured Beryl's life had probably improved. Her husband had been shiftless, never keeping a job for very long. Beryl had fallen for him in college, believing that he would make something of himself.

What he'd made of himself—and of their family, too—had been a mess. The children had seen things children should never see: fights and anger and deliberate misunderstandings. Fortunately they hadn't seen him in at least three years.

Poppy shook her head. They were such good

kids. This time they would have someone who stood by them and who thought of them first. She would raise them the way Beryl would have wanted, and she vowed not to allow herself to be swept away by her own desires.

It was a mistake too many women—and men, as Last had so honestly admitted—made.

And, as he'd said, they were completely wrong for each other.

She would take him to this ranch he called Malfunction Junction—such an odd name for a home—and then she would determine whether it was a suitable place for children.

If it was, she would apply to become a teacher in one of the public schools. That way, she could build a reputation that was solid.

She would not kiss him again.

By morning, he would forget that it had ever happened, his injuries paining him as they must.

She shouldn't have kissed him at all.

This was the case, despite the children. Last was a rogue, though a sweet one, and undeniably aware of his appeal. He was a bachelor to his core, she thought with a touch of disgust as she pulled on a T-shirt and a pair of loose pajama bottoms. "Which suits this bachelorette just fine. Be a bachelor all you like." Crawling into her bed, she sighed, enjoying the comfort she'd felt there since childhood.

"Excuse me."

She shrieked.

Last stood inside her doorway.

"Yes?" she asked, jerking the covers to her chin.

He grinned, clearly aware of her discomfort. "So prim and proper."

She raised her chin haughtily. "Thank you."

"I just want you to know that I don't mind being one of your many protective admirers. Maybe you'll accept a marriage proposal yet, but it can never be from me."

Jumping out of bed, she quickly pulled on a robe.

"Nice," he said, "though the circus costume is better."

"You must be feeling quite a bit better if you're prowling the halls. Though you're still suffering from a swollen ego," she said. "And you've been quite clear on all marital matters. As if I care."

He nodded, and suddenly the smile was gone. His eyes turned dark. "I shouldn't have kissed you," he said. "That's what I came in here to say. I make a sincere promise not to do it again."

Lovely. A man with more conscience than she possessed—and probably the strength to back it up. "Fine," she said. "I'm not exactly heartbroken, but I appreciate your burst of consideration."

Nodding, he left.

"Butthead!" she murmured.

"I heard that," he said, poking his head back into the room. "But I don't mind since I know you're under duress. Does your mother know you have such a potty mouth?"

She closed the door in his face and got back in bed. "As if I would fall for such an eighteenth-century throwback as Last Jefferson!"

Last did kiss like a dream. But he was definitely not the man for her little family.

"Butthead!" she muttered into her pillow, feeling quite satisfied that this time her admonishment had gone unheard by the cocky cowboy.

Chapter Four

Four days later Last was feeling better. He had survived several days in a truck with two kids and a very quiet woman. His body pain was mostly gone, but he had noticed a distinct and annoying side effect: mental pain.

Esme's withdrawal was bothering him. A lot.

He wanted to see her smile, hear her laugh. See her sparkle. Out of her natural conditions—and alone with him—he realized she simply did not feel like smiling.

Which was very odd, because women tended to smile a lot around him.

One more unsmiling face greeted him as he pulled up to Malfunction Junction. "Guests?" Mason asked.

"For a while." Last helped the tired kids from the

truck. Esme got out and introduced herself to Mason as Poppy.

Pacified for the moment by Esme's beauty and charm, Mason managed a smile. The children ran off to look at the pond out back, and seeing Mason's uncompromising expression, Esme quietly excused herself and followed her children.

Brother glared at brother. Mason shook his head. "What do you think you're doing?"

"I don't really know, to be honest," Last said.

"You were supposed to be on a sabbatical, not a family-finding mission."

Last sighed. "I know. Funny how I didn't get much sabbating done."

"Well, I can see the appeal, but—"

"She's not my girlfriend."

Mason's brows shot up. "So what is she?"

"Friend," Last stated.

"A friend with two children." Mason rocked back on his heels. "Do you think you need more? I know you're out of sorts now that it's just me and you at the ranch, but this may be too much."

"They're not actually her children. She's their aunt. And God only knows, Mason, if I didn't want to be alone with you, I'd just find another place on the ranch to be. I wouldn't bring home a girlfriend to relieve the animosity."

Mason's lips compressed. He shook his head and sighed. "What I want to know is when it became animosity."

"Probably about the time you came home from your own sabbatical and found yourself uncle to my unexpected child. You weren't very supportive of me at the time."

"I felt Valentine's needs had to come first. She was the mother, and you were being a donkey's hind end."

Last shrugged. He couldn't deny the truth. "All right. I'm only saying that's probably when the animosity began. I've never liked holier-than-thou routines."

"Well, if you'd properly employed the Condom Song—"

"Mason," Last said, "what's it like to be so staunch? So right all the time? So perfect?"

Mason looked at him for another long moment, then turned on his heel and went inside.

"Now *that's* animosity," Last said. He went off to find Esme, who sat forlornly on a bench under one of the many willow trees that had been planted around the pond by his brother Tex.

The fact was, Last hadn't known how much he was willing to protect this woman and her brood until Mason decided to dog them out. Something feral and intense had stirred to life inside Last that he couldn't yet put a name to. But he knew it wasn't going away.

"Hey," he said.

She looked up. "I've got it figured out. Your brother doesn't want us here."

"So? Mason's got a stick up his butt. He always has. Forget about it."

"How did it get there?"

Last rolled his eyes. "When he let the woman he loved slip away. Pay him no mind. None of us do." Mason's heavy-handedness had grated on all the brothers' nerves, giving each one a reason to find his own path, leading away from Malfunction Junction. Last stayed behind on the ranch because of his young daughter. "Most of my brothers have left. I'd be gone, too," he said, "but I became a father."

"Well, that speaks very well of you," Esme said.

He looked at her. Her dark hair gleamed in the sunlight, and she wore no makeup except lip gloss. He thought she was the most beautiful woman he'd ever seen. "I'm sorry I hurt your feelings the other night," he said softly.

"You…oh, all right," she capitulated. "I was going to deny it, but you did."

He nodded. "I'll probably do that a lot. It seems to be something I do."

She gave him an even look. "Stop doing it."

"It's a Jefferson trait."

Shrugging, she said, "Grow a different gene. I challenge you."

This woman would not give him a break. He watched the kids playing on the deck, staring into the water, looking for whatever it was California kids found so fascinating about a Texas pond. "Anything for you," he said finally, knowing he meant it.

She turned her head to watch Curtis and Amelia. "I'm sorry we got you into trouble, but thank you for bringing us here. I can tell they're going to love Malfunction Junction."

He hoped so. Or maybe he was just an idiot for bringing them here. Maybe Mason was partially right about Last wanting a buffer between him and his older brother.

But the real buffer he needed was between him and his wayward heart. "I'm glad you're here," he said sincerely. "Thanks for doing me the favor."

She smiled at him. "Yeah."

They sat there for a few minutes, soaking in the setting sun and the joy of the children running around the pond.

"Last?"

Turning, he saw Valentine walking toward him with Annette in her arms. "Hey, baby!" He jumped up to grab his daughter, kissing her face with joy. "You've grown!"

Valentine looked at Esme before returning her gaze to Last. "You were gone less than two weeks. She couldn't have grown."

"Then my heart grew for you," he told Annette. "Valentine, this is…Poppy Peabody. Poppy, Valentine, wife to my brother Crockett." Hesitating, Last decided it was time to get real; it was time to begin telling the truth with no playacting to cover it up. "Actually," he said slowly, looking at Poppy, "her name is Esme Hastings, which I think is beautiful."

"Hello, Esme," Valentine said quietly. "It's nice to meet you."

Valentine's reaction startled him more than Mason's had. He couldn't understand what the big deal was. They'd had twenty women here before, during the big storm, and women stayed over at the ranch for many other reasons, too. The Jeffersons always took care of each other and of anyone else that needed caring for. How was this different?

Crockett lumbered over, giving Last a hearty slap on the back. "So soon the prodigal son returns," he said.

"Shut up, Crockett," Last said. "This is Esme Hastings. Esme, meet one of the dirty dozen."

Crockett grinned at Esme. "Welcome."

"Well, we must be going," Valentine said. "It's good to meet you, Esme. Last is right. Esme is a lovely name. Very elegant." She took Annette from Last, casting an eye toward the children playing around the pond. "Your children?" she asked.

"Niece and nephew."

"Oh." Valentine smiled. "Bring them to my bakery sometime after you get more settled in. Where are you staying, by the way?"

Reluctantly Last said, "In the house you moved out of."

"Oh." Valentine nodded after a moment. "Well, you'll find it very comfortable. Goodbye."

She walked away with Crockett, and Last sighed. Esme looked at him. "Guess that was awkward for you."

"Everything about this family is awkward for

me." He sighed again, deciding to unload some of his feelings. "I'm the youngest of twelve, and even in school I was looked at as the last of the Jefferson boys. It was almost as if teachers expected me to tear things up and make mischief. Follow in the family footsteps."

"And did you?"

"Of course," Last said, "although much more responsibly than my brothers. But then I made one teensy little lapse in judgment—"

"And a cute thing she is," Esme said with a smile.

"And suddenly I'm the brother everybody rags on."

"Actually I bet it's because all the rest of them are married now. You're the loner, except for Mason. And because you're his kid brother, there's a pretty wide gulf there."

He looked at her. "I never thought of it that way."

"And Valentine just didn't know what to think about another woman being around her child. I completely understand that."

"Yeah," Last said slowly. "I know that feeling, too."

"They'll settle down after they get to know me."

Last blinked. "Make me a promise."

"Oh, I really don't make promises to men," Esme said. "I don't seem to be able to keep them very well."

"Keep this one to me. Promise me you won't leave me here alone with them."

She laughed. "They're your family. And they seem very nice."

"Our friendship is good for me," he said, meaning it. "You give me deeper perception."

"Of what?"

"My life."

She looked at him uncertainly. "You seem fine to me."

"So promise, if I seem so fine."

"I can't." She shook her head. "I have to think of the children."

That was true. He would agree that children came first, above all. "At least tell me if you decide you're not happy here."

"I will." Esme smiled at him. "I'm only here for a month, at first, anyway."

He remembered the elderly man sitting next to him at the circus. "The judge is quite conservative. We'll have to consider your battle plan."

She laughed. "I don't need a battle plan. We're here in the land of stability, right?"

He shook his head. "As you can see, it's more Malfunction Junction."

"So it's always awkward?"

"It's always…family."

Esme nodded. "Then it's fine with me."

"Esme," he said suddenly, taking her hand, "I know this is going to sound bizarre, but I think you belong here."

She blinked. "You're only saying that because my presence annoys your family."

He grinned. "That certainly is a point in your favor. However, I really do think you will like Union Junction."

"Because?"

He let his gaze roam over her face, marveling at its texture and delicate lines. "I just hope you do," he said softly. "I think you'd make a great addition to the family."

"Too bad all the brothers are hitched," she said. "Except for Mason—"

"Don't even think about it," Last said. "As it is, I may have to protect you from any loose cowboys in town. While you're here, you are under my protection, you know."

She raised a brow. "Protection?"

He nodded. "Exactly. It's the least I can do."

"So when do you leave to go bungee jumping?"

He wondered at the abrupt question. She'd turned her head from him, showing him a profile that gave nothing away.

And that's when he knew that his heart was going in a direction neither of them wanted. He was just like the lion tamer, the ringmaster and the man in the gorilla suit, offering something she might need but didn't want.

"Soon," he said. "Come on. Let me show you to your temporary digs."

"FORBIDDEN FRUIT is not really safe to eat," Mason said when Last went inside the main ranch house later that day.

"Forbidden?" Last looked at his eldest brother. "What the hell are you talking about?"

"I have a funny feeling that woman is carrying a bit of baggage with her," Mason said.

Last looked at his stern brother. "Doesn't everybody we know?"

"You're not planning on anything serious with her, are you?"

"No." Last shook his head. "I'm not planning anything serious in my life at all."

"Damn it!" Mason thundered. "That's your whole problem! Nothing is serious for you!"

Resenting Mason's fatherly approach, Last turned away. "I'm serious about Annette."

"Then don't introduce a woman into her life you know nothing about."

Last stiffened. Just Mason's tone made him want to go kiss the daylights out of Esme. He was hot for her. He wanted her like crazy, though he denied it to everyone and mostly to himself. All of the questions and doubts Mason had about her had already occurred to Last, but they'd been subsumed by the magic that had come over him the moment he laid eyes on her at the beach.

"Mason, shut the hell up," Last said suddenly. "It's time you put your nose in your own business and kept it out of mine."

Mason stared at him, his brows etched tightly together, but Last wasn't worried about Mason's thundering attitude. "I don't care what you think." Last said quietly. "She's a good woman. Those are good kids. If they're not welcome here, then they'll go, but so will I."

Mason's eyes grew dark. "Then this time use protection."

Last walked to within an inch of his brother.

"Mason, if you ever say anything like that to me again, I swear you'll lose a brother for good."

With those words, Last faced down Mason for the first time in his life. And Last knew he was finally starting to grow up.

Chapter Five

Poppy relaxed at Malfunction Junction over the next week. She and the children settled in and they got to know Olivia and Calhoun and their children, Minnie and Kenny. Curtis and Amelia loved riding Gypsy and couldn't believe their new friends had a wonderful windmill in their yard.

There was much about the ranch that fit Poppy and the children just fine, but there was just as much that was uncomfortable. Poppy laid out clothes for the children to wear to their first day of school, wanting them to look their best. She had enrolled them as quickly as possible, deciding that it was time for them to enjoy a different type of education than they had heretofore.

It was also time for her to seek employment. Dressing herself with care—and trying to look as little like the seductress Mason clearly thought she was—Poppy went to the high school and applied for a job teaching English grammar and the classics.

To her surprise, the principal was more than happy to hire her, on the condition that she got her Texas teaching certificate. "It's not often we get a double major with a master's degree applying here," the principal said. "Your life experience is textured and unique, and I'm interested in your doctoral project."

Poppy shook her head. "I don't know that I'll ever finish."

The principal nodded. "It will be a challenge with the parenting role you've undertaken. However, I have no doubt that one day I will address you as Dr. Hastings."

Poppy walked out into the sunlight of the waning August day, feeling as if she floated on air without benefit of pulleys and circus equipment. "Dr. Esmerelda Hastings," she murmured, liking her name for the first time in her life. "Esme."

In fact, she really liked the person she was becoming.

She was changing, and a lot of the positive change was due to Last. He'd been the first one to call her Esme, and she was beginning to feel as if the exotic, beautiful name fit her. When she reached the truck she'd borrowed from the Jeffersons' ranch, Curtis and Amelia hopped out of the back.

"How did it go?" Amelia asked.

"Believe it or not, I have a job. I'll be working in a school very close to yours." Esme smiled. "I can hardly believe it!"

The children clapped, their joy obvious.

"I like it here," Curtis said. "Let's stay for always!"

Amelia grew serious. "Did you tell the principal that we have to go back to California in a month?"

Poppy...Esme nodded. "She has a substitute already. It will take time for me to get my teaching certificate renewed and updated for Texas education anyway. There's a great deal of work I have to do and training to go through. I won't actually put in my first day of school until December, although I can substitute once I get my certification."

"That's wonderful, Aunt Poppy," Amelia said.

"Aunt Esme now," she said with a smile.

"Why?" Curtis asked.

"Last thinks we should all be who we really are." She smiled as she got into the driver's side, the children getting in the passenger side. "I have to say there's something very relaxing about being who I really am."

Curtis looked at her as he put on his seat belt. "Are you going to marry Last?"

Esme shook her head as she started the truck. "No. But he's a good friend."

"We wouldn't mind if you did," Amelia said.

"We've never had a father before," Curtis said. "Not a real father, anyway."

Amelia nodded. "He's spent more time with us than—"

"It's okay," Esme said. "Don't think about the past. Just be happy."

"We do worry," Amelia said. "It's not as easy as waving a wand."

Esme stopped the truck, turning to look at the kids' worried faces.

"We really like it here," Curtis said softly, his slightly freckled face earnest and hopeful.

"I know you do. We'll try to make it work as best we can." Esme touched both of their faces for an instant. "Be brave. I know it's hard, but I'm positive it will all work out for the best."

"There's no magic in Malfunction Junction," Amelia said. "It's like you're a superhero who can't use your powers."

"Which is scary," Curtis added.

"Hmm," Esme said. "You're right. Definitely no

sleight of hand and no illusion will work here. However, we'll just have to be ourselves and let that be magic enough."

The kids nodded, sitting back in their seats. Okay, she was scared, too, but it would do no good to voice her worries. They had to make the most of this wonderful opportunity Last had given them.

He'd asked her not to leave and so had the children. She would try her hardest to make it work—for all of them.

"YOU'VE GOT TO LET GO," Mimi told Mason. "All that anger isn't healthy."

Mason gazed at his best friend, the biggest source of trouble, heartbreak and joy in his life. "I want to kick his tail."

Mimi put the final touches on an apple pie for her father, the former sheriff of Union Junction, and took off her apron. "Mason, Last had to grow up one day. Only Peter Pan remained a boy forever, and I'm not so sure that was healthy."

"At least he could fly." Mason was disgruntled and determined to gripe about everything.

"Apparently so could Esme. The circus must have been an interesting place to live."

"I have always hated the circus. Clowns bother me."

Mimi laughed. "Oh, please. You always spent so much time around the rodeo. Calhoun married a rodeo clown's daughter. And let us not forget, the Jefferson boys had some clownish moments of their own." She looked at him. "Mason, you're going to have to accept that your baby brother has grown up."

Mason pursed his lips. Only Mimi dared to reveal the naked truth to him. He appreciated it—and it made him mad as hell. She was sass and good sense. She bent over to look at something in the oven, and his gaze settled on her sexy rear end for a split second before he forced himself to look away.

"I just don't like her," he said. "She's odd."

"She's exotic," Mimi said, standing. "And would you expect anything less from one of your brothers? I don't think any of them have married a boring girl."

Mason didn't like that either. "It upset Valentine."

"And she got over it. She was surprised, Mason, that's all. Perfectly normal, don't you think? Not worth writing a dramatic script over."

"Mimi," Mason said, "you're annoying me."

"Good. Someone needs to."

The apple pie smelled heavenly, and that did

nothing to improve his mood. The sheriff's and Nanette's dinners also smelled good. Mason frowned, his stomach rumbling. Helga, the ranch's housekeeper, was a good cook, but sometime when he wasn't looking, Mimi had developed a talent for delightful home cooking. He almost always could find a reason to perch in her kitchen, hoping to snag a snack.

He worked and he went there to see Mimi's daughter Nanette and fill his belly. It was a good life, though there was still something missing.

"My family is a pain in my ass," he said suddenly.

"And you really need to get over that, too," Mimi said. "It's nearly all over. They all have their own families. Then what will you gripe about?"

Mason scratched his head, wondering why he always felt so unsettled. "I'll find something."

"You know," she said, putting a beer in front of him, "you weren't always such a drag."

Mason blinked. "Wasn't I?"

"No. You used to be fun. We used to have wonderful adventures."

His gaze flicked for the slightest instant to the blouse that stuck nicely to her body. Motherhood definitely agreed with her. "You dragged me into them."

"You only lacked imagination."

"That's supposed to make me feel better?" He drank his beer, realizing that somehow Mimi had coaxed him out of his dismay over Last's newest familial additions. "Damn it, I never had time to have an imagination."

"Well, now you do. You'll have lots of time, and surely there is fertile ground residing inside that handsome head of yours."

"Mimi, do you ever hear from Brian?" Mason asked suddenly, wondering how her ex-husband had ever let her go.

Her gaze separated from his. She turned to check something on the stove. "No. We're on good terms, but we have no reason to talk to each other."

"What about Nanette?" Mason asked. "I always thought Brian was a pretty good ol' guy. It surprises me that he doesn't want to see his daughter."

Mimi shrugged but didn't look at him. "Some men are better at fathering than others."

"I guess." Mason stood. "Thanks for the supper, Mimi."

She didn't meet his gaze. "You're welcome."

He realized he'd hurt her feelings, and that was the last thing he wanted to do to his childhood friend and confidante. Walking to her, he lifted her chin gently. "Sorry," he said gruffly. "I shouldn't have brought it up."

Mimi gazed up at him, her blue eyes sparkling with tears. His heart grew tight inside him. "I'm a jerk," he said. "You were happy until I came here with my problems and my big mouth."

Mimi nodded. "Yes, you are a jerk," she said softly. "But…I still think you should run for sheriff."

Smiling, he pulled away from her. "That's my Mimi. Always looking for the next adventure." He kissed her cheek lightly, tipped his hat and left the kitchen to go say goodbye to the sheriff and Nanette.

Mimi being Mimi, she really was the only woman who could make him feel as if he was still a cowboy who mattered.

"IT JUST CAUGHT ME by surprise is all," Valentine said to Last as he came to her bakery, Baked Valentines, to drop off Annette. "I wasn't expecting you to bring home a souvenir family. Esme seems perfectly lovely, though."

"I wasn't expecting it either. One moment I was in the air, hanging by some fabric and good luck, and the next thing I knew…"

"You were falling for a woman and her children." Valentine smiled. "Sounds very romantic."

"No," Last said, "it's not like that. I didn't fall for her, and she certainly didn't for me. It's not romantic at all."

Valentine looked at him as she put in a sheet of cookies. "Did Esme tell you she came by here after she applied at the school?"

Last frowned. "Applied at the school?"

Valentine hesitated. "Perhaps I shouldn't be such a gossip."

"No." Last shook his head. "When did this happen?"

"A few days ago. She applied and was accepted, though she has training to do, of course. Then she brought the children here. I gave them a snack, and Esme and I had a long girl chat. It was fun." Valentine shrugged. "There's something about her that really is quite innocent and refreshing."

"She doesn't tell me anything," Last said. "Why doesn't she have a girl chat with me?"

"Because you're not a girl?" Valentine said. "And maybe she'd like a bit of independence? Jefferson males can be quite claustrophobic with their...you know."

"No, I don't." Last was growing more irritated by the moment. Why hadn't Esme told him she'd applied for a job? Instead she'd stopped by to see the mother of his child.

"Well, their machismo," Valentine said. "You brothers all have a healthy dose of it. Sometimes it's romantic, sometimes it's amusing—and sometimes it's annoying."

"I still think she should tell me things." Last didn't like this new private side of Esme. It made him feel less in control of… "We have no relationship," he said slowly.

"I know," Valentine said, surprised. "You told me."

"I guess she doesn't owe me anything."

"No. Not even a daily accounting of her whereabouts." Valentine shrugged. "I thought it was brave and admirable of her to go out in a town she knows nothing about and seek employment. It shows that she's not looking for a Mrs. degree."

Last tightened his lips. "I never thought she was taking advantage of me. And we both agreed in the beginning that we were totally wrong for each other. I was only trying to help her out."

"Sure," Valentine said, "and these cookies are all going to jump in the oven themselves. Get up off your duff and start putting some trays in ovens."

He complied, glad at that moment for Valentine's direction. "Mason thinks she's got too much baggage for me."

"No." Valentine shook her head. "She has more life experience maybe. Why?" She looked at him, a twinkle in her eye. "I thought Esme was only someone you rescued."

"Actually she rescued me from a sea lion," Last said. "I really was out of my element in California."

"So when do you leave on your African bungee tour?"

The idea was less appealing than it had been a few weeks ago. "I'm not sure."

Valentine grinned as he burned his hand on an oven. "Last, you have a woman on your mind."

He grunted, not about to agree.

"Anyway, I wouldn't let anything Mason has to say about a woman influence you." Valentine shook her head. "He doesn't appear to be a romance expert, does he?"

"Hell, no. And I'm not looking for romance," he insisted. "I was only commenting that Mason thought Esme had more experience than me."

"Only in terms of maturity," Valentine said, turning to peer into the oven. "But you've grown up a ton since I met you."

Annoyed, Last stood. "Thanks for the advice. I'll be by tomorrow to get Annette."

"All right," she said absently, not looking at him, her gaze still on the cookies. Last nodded, putting his hat on his head.

He needed to have a chat with Miss Esme, he decided. He would initiate this girl-chat session, and she would tell him everything she'd told Valentine.

Then maybe he wouldn't have this unsettled feeling.

He wanted her to need him as much as he needed her.

"THE CHILDREN WONDERED why you didn't come by today." Esme smiled at Last, letting him in the front door. "You missed the small supper I fixed."

"You've settled in quickly." Last looked around the den. "This looks different."

"We're used to setup and takedown in the circus. We simply moved some things around to make it homier for us. The children and I like to play cards, and the sofa was too close to the TV."

She gauged his mood to be somewhat down. "Sit," she said. "The kids are in bed, but I'll get you some of the dinner we ate."

"No, thank you," he said. "Let's just sit here and you can tell me what you've been up to."

"I actually feel like a glass of tea," Esme said, suddenly nervous. His mood was so formal and almost stiff! "And I haven't been up to much. Just applying for a job, and I stopped in to see Valentine. She'd invited us, you know, and so we went, because the children wanted a snack and they'd never been inside the back of a bakery—"

She stopped talking as he took the tea glass from her hand. "What is it?"

"I don't know," he said. "I've been denying the truth for days, but I think I'm going to go crazy if I don't kiss you."

Then he did kiss her, and against her better judgment, Esme let him take her in his arms. He felt just as good as she remembered—better, even—and the fact was, she liked it when he kissed her.

He kissed her hard and fast, and in that instant Esme realized Last wanted her in the way she had never let another man want her. "Kiss me more," she said.

"Are the children really asleep?" he asked against her neck.

"Completely tuckered out."

He picked her up and carried her down the hall

to her bedroom. Esme laid her head against his chest, feeling nervous and excited all at once.

"I was lying to myself. I didn't come here for girl chat," Last murmured, laying her on the bed. "I came here for something totally different."

"What?" she asked, staring up at him as he looked down at her.

"I think I came here to learn who you really are," he said.

Esme's heart beat so hard she could feel it in her neck. "Just what you see," she said.

"Then I want to see more."

She reached out her arms to him. "Hurry," she whispered. "You don't want to miss the show no one's ever seen."

He locked the door, stripped off his clothes and boots, getting into bed. "You're still dressed," he said.

She pulled her dress over her head. "Now I'm not."

He unfastened her bra, shoved down her panties and kissed her so hotly Esme thought she was going to scream with pleasure. His hands were everywhere, touching her, stroking her.

"Say yes," he told her.

She wasn't about to say no, no matter what reservations she'd had on their trip to Texas. "Right now," she said urgently. "Don't make me wait."

When he slid inside her, she tensed with pain.

Last hesitated, looking down at her, a surprised expression on his face. "That's not the usual reaction from a woman."

"I'm sorry," she said. "I wasn't expecting pain either."

He gazed at her, his eyes suddenly clearing. "Oh, my God," he said. "Why didn't you tell me you're a virgin?"

"It's not important, is it?" She was very afraid he'd stop and leave her, and she so much wanted him to stay exactly where he was.

"It's important," Last said, moving gently inside her, kissing her deeply, his hands stroking her so that she relaxed. Last grinned, slow and sexy. He held her close to him, rocking her, and she let him work his magic, and all thoughts flew out of her head until all she could think about was Last and how wonderful he made her feel.

Suddenly waves of pleasure washed over her. Esme climaxed, and it was better than the best show under the big top. "Don't stop," she said on a moan. "Don't ever stop."

Last kissed her, taking her lips with his, and

she knew the second he found his own pleasure. Warmth flooded her at knowing that she gave him happiness. They lay together for a long time holding each other, and it was only when she awakened and he was gone that Esme realized they hadn't used any protection at all.

Chapter Six

Last Jefferson knew he was in big trouble.

Moreover, he might have gotten Esme into big trouble, a fact that made his heart sink.

He had not expected her to be a virgin. In fact, he'd listened to Mason's drivel about her being more experienced. The logical conclusion was that she was using precautionary measures. He hoped.

In his need to possess her, he hadn't really been listening to her. He hadn't gotten to know her.

And if the judge objected to her showgirl magician lifestyle, he'd really protest her becoming a pregnant single mother.

Last felt ill. "This one is all my fault," he said, staring at the rows of fence he'd been working on all morning. Fence repair was good for him. Lonely and solitary and time-consuming, it gave him a chance to think about the roller coaster his life had become.

One day he'd been floating through the sky, escaping from his problems, and the next thing he knew, he was flying straight into something that couldn't be easily resolved.

He owed Esme a lot better than he'd given her.

"Hey," Calhoun said, riding up to him. "What are you doing?"

"What does it look like?"

"Moping?" Calhoun asked.

Last glanced up at his brother. "If you already knew, then why'd you ask?"

Calhoun laughed, getting down to hold the roll of wire so Last could clip it more easily. "This is what I do when I need to think."

"Well, I'm not really thinking."

"You were thinking so hard you didn't hear Gypsy and me ride up."

Last shrugged.

"I like your girlfriend."

"Esme's not my…whatever," Last said on a sigh.

"Saw your truck there late last night," Calhoun offered. "Mason did, too."

"Oh, hell." Last didn't need Mason deciding to

give him another big-brother butt-kicking. "I am really starting to hate the ranch."

"It can be claustrophobic," Calhoun agreed.

"No, just Mason."

"Yeah. Well, he's going through the change."

Last glanced up. "The change of what?"

"Attitude."

"You must be joking."

"Sure. He's trying to figure out what he's going to do with all this. We're going to have to hire help if you ship off to California."

Last stared at Calhoun. "Why the hell would I do that?"

Calhoun shrugged. "Same reason your truck was parked outside Esme's late last night?"

Last rolled his eyes, accidentally clipping his finger. "Damn it!"

Calhoun sat on the ground, giving up the wire to look at his brother. "I'm sorry you're the last one here."

"I'm sorry I'm the last one, period. I'm sorry I'm Last. It sucks." He chafed having everybody in his business. Nobody could understand what was between him and Esme—he didn't even understand it himself. But he wanted time to explore it without the circus of his family intruding. "Hey, I know you mean well, but butt out, okay?"

Calhoun sighed. "Sure."

Last grunted, sucking the blood off his finger and clipping the next wire. Doggedly he clipped and attached, ignoring Calhoun. After a while his brother got up and rode away in silence. Last shook his head. He was now about two miles from the house, and the farther away he got, the happier he was.

Maybe that was all he needed. Distance.

Twenty minutes later, just about the time he felt as if he couldn't clip another wire, he heard, "Hey."

Glancing up, he saw Esme in a pretty cotton dress, holding a picnic basket and a patio umbrella. "Hey," he said, happier than he wanted to be that she was there. "How'd you know where I was?"

"Your brother said you needed a bandage." She handed him a foil condom packet. "I found this one in a nightstand in the other bedroom when I was unpacking the children's clothes."

"This isn't a bandage." Last watched her open the umbrella and spread it behind them so that they were shielded from the ranch's view. She carefully laid a blanket on the ground and set the picnic basket on it. He already had an erection, so she was making him very, very nervous.

"Depends on what kind of bandage you need." Esme stood, and her long white skirt billowed around her in the breeze. "What did you hurt?"

Mainly his pride. "Esme, I'm sorry about last night," he said. "My schmuck potential is pretty high—off the charts, actually. I should have taken—"

"It's fine," she said. "I'm pretty sure there'll be no surprises—for you, me or the judge. However," she said, "you and I still have something to discuss."

He watched with interest as she approached him, her hands reaching for his belt. "I'm open to all discussions."

She undid his jeans. "Good. I was hoping you'd say that, because there's a lot we haven't talked about."

God, he hoped she had more than talking on her mind. He was about to lose his cool and pounce on her. "Name the subject."

She gently pushed him back on the blanket and eased him from his jeans. Lifting her skirt, she took the condom from him, slipping it over him. He nearly exploded when she sank down on top of him.

"This is definitely the best lunch I've ever been served," he said on a hoarse gasp.

"Hold me," she said, and he did. They sat together, her legs over his, connected in the most intimate fashion. He put his face against her hair, smelling the fragrance of her.

"You feel wonderful," he said, his brain on fire.

"I needed to know if last night was a one-time thing." She moved on him, just barely, so that they would be more tightly locked together.

"I don't think so," he said, his throat tight. "I don't think I could leave you alone to save my life." He sneaked his hands under her skirt, holding her bare, smooth bottom in his hands. A groan escaped him, so she kissed him, her hands gently holding his face. He squeezed her so that he could feel her more tightly around him, then he slowly moved her back and forth. "God, it's good," he said on an appreciative groan. "Stay on me forever."

She giggled. "I can't. Eventually I have to feed the children."

He looked at her in alarm. "Where are they?"

"Shh," she said, kissing his mouth. "They're at Olivia's playing with Minnie and Kenny. You're totally safe."

Until she moved again, and then he felt in grave danger of climaxing before he pleased her. He buried his face in her breasts, feeling her all around him, the most wonderful sensation he could ever imagine. He let her move him the way she liked best, and when she climaxed, he rolled her over so that she lay beneath him.

"I love your eyes," he said, watching her enjoy their lovemaking as he moved inside her more deeply. "They tell me everything you're thinking."

Right now she was thinking he was magic, so he showed her exactly what real magic was, bringing her to a second climax, this one loud enough to startle a pheasant from a nearby patch of grass.

"Wow," he said, biting at her neck, "here I thought you were such a quiet girl."

"Maybe." She crossed her legs over his back, sinking him deep inside her. He gasped, then tensed, his whole body bucking beyond his control. When his climax hit, it took his breath so that he collapsed against Esme, his body shaking.

"Wow," Esme said, her voice a giggle in his ear. "You made mine sound insignificant. Let's do this every day."

He groaned against her neck, wanting to be hard immediately. "I will if you will."

"Picnic lunch?"

"Absolutely," he said. "This is a big ranch, and we can picnic in every square inch of it." Raising up on an arm, he looked down into her face. "Except we can't once you start working."

"Then you can bring lunch to me," she said.

He *was* feeling himself get hard inside her again. "Tell me more about these working lunches," he said. "Isn't it too soon after moving here for you to go to work?"

"How else will I earn money? Besides, I'm excited about teaching."

He looked at the wild gypsy beneath him, knowing he was never going to tame her. "Could you at least discuss your plans with me ahead of time?"

"No," Esme said.

He put a palm around one of her breasts, squeezing the nipple lightly.

"Maybe," she said. "If you try not to be so bossy."

"But I am bossy." He moved inside her, suddenly realizing she was an itch he might not ever fully scratch.

"Last," Esme said. "I have to go."

He didn't want her to. "Why?"

"My kids. And this condom is pretty shot, I'm certain. As little as I know about condoms, I think they may only be good for one time."

Reluctantly, he agreed. "Next picnic, bring two."

She scrambled up from the ground, sweeping her hair away from her face. "I was only supposed to bring you a bandage. Don't complain."

"I intend to thank Calhoun for sending you." Last watched her pack up her picnic basket with interest. "Hey, I didn't get any of that."

"Oh. This is for the children," she said, picking up the umbrella as she rose to her feet. "You can bring the blanket back. Goodbye!"

She left, her white eyelet skirt billowing around her legs. Every part of his body was happy, except perhaps his heart.

She was definitely testing his vow to stay a single father forever. It was clear that she was a forgiving, understanding, hot-blooded creature…and yet he knew she'd been honest about there being no possible future between them.

He should be devoting most of his time and energies toward his relationship with his daughter anyway. He should just enjoy the sex—with proper precautions, he thought, looking at the clouds floating overhead like free spirits.

But for some reason, he had the nagging feeling that his best bet for happiness would be to earn a place in Esme's heart.

"IT'S GOOD TO SEE YOU, Mr. Jefferson," Principal Carrol said.

Last stopped himself from wringing the cowboy hat he held in his hands. Something about Principal Carrol had always made him nervous, from kindergarten through graduation. He wasn't certain why. She had such kindly eyes and an even gentler demeanor.

"What can I do for you?" she asked. "Your daughter won't be coming to school here for a few more years."

He nodded. "Yes. That's right. But I believe a friend of mine applied for a job here. Esmerelda Hastings."

Mrs. Carrol smiled. "Quite fortunate we are to have her knowledge and experience in our country high school. She will be an asset."

The urge to squirm was strong. He knew well his reputation and that of his brothers. Yet if anything, Esme had shown him that lives were not irreversible. "I wonder if my skills would be an asset as well."

Mrs. Carrol looked over her glasses at him. "Yours?"

"As a teacher," he said. "I realize that only two

languages are taught here for the students of Union Junction, French and Spanish. Our father was very big on our education—"

"We are aware that you boys were in school for the social and entertainment value," Mrs. Carrol said with a wink. "Though we take some credit for the fact that you eventually turned out to be contributing members of society."

"Well, that's just it," Last said. "I haven't really contributed."

Mrs. Carrol nodded. "Of all the Jeffersons, you'd be the one I'd be most pleased to have here as a teacher."

"Really?" Last was surprised. "I always felt I was in eleven shadows."

"You were. But you were by far the best student. Much more intent. Weren't you called the family philosopher?"

"Yes, but my brothers weren't being complimentary," Last said.

"You didn't throw yourself into mischief with the same enthusiasm that they and Mimi did," Mrs. Carrol said with a smile.

"But I was no saint."

"No," she said, "but you seemed to only half-heartedly try to keep up the family reputation.

Frankly I estimated you to be the brother who went the farthest in life."

His brows rose. "No one has ever said that to me before."

She smiled. "Sometimes you have to ask a teacher to get a correct answer."

He took a deep breath. "I really would like to teach here, if you could use me."

"Last, you received an education most people will never receive outside of a private academy. I am certain the school would benefit from Latin courses—"

"College preparatory," he inserted. "Serious, college-bound students."

She nodded. "Understood. I will put the topic in front of the school board and let them vote."

"I don't need compensation," Last said. "It's time I gave something back, and this would be a labor of my heart."

"You'll have to get your certification. Other than that, I can't see anything standing in your way." She hesitated for a moment. "Latin teachers are not easy to find, particularly good ones. I presume you know you could most likely get a job at a university or a community college and do far better than here in Union Junction."

"Maybe," Last said, "but this is my town."

"And Miss Hastings will be here."

He shook his head. "She gave me the idea—and maybe the realization of what I needed in my life—but Miss Hastings and I are not destined for the altar."

She shrugged. "I did wonder, as you brought her here. Confidentially, the math teacher was asking about her…marital status."

Tickling started up the back of Last's scalp. "Single. And likely to stay that way, from what I know."

"I was curious as to what made you bring Miss Hastings with you. It's far for her to travel, isn't it?" She checked some paperwork in front of her. "All of her credentials are sterling. Recommendations from college professors mostly, from Harvard."

He stared at his old principal. "Harvard?"

She nodded. "Yes. Born in Britain, graduated from Harvard."

"Not…ringmasters or lion tamers? Magician types?"

Mrs. Carrol laughed. "Not as far as any paperwork indicates—and we are quite thorough for the protection of our students. I can't say any more about Miss Hastings than I have. I thought you knew her."

He sat silently, his heart beating. "I thought I did," he said, "but I believe it was a famous philosopher who once said that cow patties fall quickly when dropped on slow boots."

"That was not a famous philosopher," she said with a grin. "It was your father."

"I'm going to spank Ms. Hastings," Last said.

"Oh, my," Mrs. Carrol said. She hid a smile behind her hand. "Do we have another Mimi Cannady living in Union Junction?"

Last got up to leave. "Expect my résumé soon and my certification as fast as I am eligible. I am quite serious about undertaking this venture."

"Your father was one of the smartest men I ever met," she said. "And you were one of my very best students, by far the best of the Jeffersons. You just needed some seasoning, which it appears you have received. I'll be waiting for you to join the staff of Union Junction High School and I'll consider a full-fledged Latin department a feather in our cap."

"Thank you, Mrs. Carrol," he said, clapping his hat firmly on his head.

"Light on the spanking," she murmured. "That is our new English lit and grammar teacher."

He shook his head, almost too irritated with Esme to cap his temper.

She had *not* been honest. And if she couldn't be honest about who she was, then he didn't intend to waste another second with her.

In fact, he considered himself much better off without her. Born in Britain? Educated at Harvard?

It explained a lot about her, most particularly the Mary Poppins behavior.

"Oh," he said out loud. "Of course. Poppy. Mary Poppins. The prim, proper British governess who loved to fly and take care of children and consorted with chimney sweeps with gymnastic ability, but who never stayed in one place very long. Just great. Dummy," he told himself.

Mason had been right. Esme—Miss Poppy— was not to be trusted. It had been much safer to live the cliché he'd been living before he'd met her.

Emotionally scarred and distrusting was so much safer than stupidly in lust.

He felt betrayed. Valentine had deceived him, too, but in a sort of after-the-fact manner, and he hadn't been falling for her. He hadn't even remembered her.

Perhaps that was why Esme hurt him so much more: she was deceiving him while stealing his heart.

Chapter Seven

Esme had known from the moment she'd driven into town, with its endless land and lush vitality, that she'd come to a wonderful place where time had slowed down. The children could be children here, and she could settle down. The land spoke to her in a way she'd never experienced before, and she was ready to listen.

Then there was Last, who was determined to talk her into giving over her heart.

She was almost ready to listen to him, too.

The children were sitting in chairs at the Union Junction salon, being attended by a covey of hairdressers, while Esme looked on. It had been a long time since either child's hair had seen a pair of scissors, and apparently it was rare that these ladies got to work with children. Everyone was enjoying the experience.

Esme decided small-town life was heaven for her and her small family.

"Beatrice, Daisy, Gretchen, Jessica, Mamie, Tisha, Velvet and Violet. That's our gang," Lily Johnston, née Bartholomew, said, sweeping her hand around the room.

"Last said there were a lot of you." She accepted a lemonade from Lily and smiled.

Daisy came and sat next to her. "So what about Mr. Jefferson?"

"Meaning?" Esme hedged, realizing she was in for a bit of well-meaning gossip.

"Is he behaving?"

The girls giggled. Esme felt herself blush. "He's very kind to the children and very nice to me. I can't say that he's been anything but a gentleman."

The stylists nodded.

"Has he taken you to Lonely Hearts Station yet?" Gretchen asked.

"Or to Barmaid's Creek?" Velvet asked.

"Shh," Tisha said. "Velvet! Really!"

"Barmaid's Creek?" Esme repeated uncomfortably.

"Don't let them tease you," Lily said. "It's just a watering hole folks sometimes like to swim in."

"Skinny dip," Mamie said. "And romance beside."

"No." Esme shook her head. "He has not taken me to Barmaid's Creek."

"We all used to live in Lonely Hearts Station," Lily explained. "With Delilah Honeycutt, who ran a salon there. She's since moved out this way."

"Two salons?" Esme asked.

"No, Delilah is doing something different now, after Valentine accidentally set Delilah's kitchen on fire," Lily said. "That was what made Delilah reevaluate what she wanted to do. Fortunately there are lots of places in Union Junction for her to choose from. They just need renovating and a bit of love and then they'd be quite homey."

Esme sat up. "That is exactly what I'm looking for. I need to find a house that I can turn into a home."

Every stylist's ear seemed to prick up at that.

"Really?" Lily said. "Aren't you happy at Malfunction Junction?"

Esme nodded. "It's very nice. But I have parents I want to move down here, and my children need a place of their own. I do, too. We can't live off the Jeffersons' generosity forever."

"Oh." Lily nodded. "I guess I'd feel the same way."

"If you and Last aren't an item," Beatrice said, "which we all assumed you were."

The women turned to stare at Beatrice.

"What?" Beatrice said. "We do think that."

"Not everything needs to be said," Jessica told her, "especially with c-h-i-l-d-r-e-n in the room."

Fully capable of deciphering that, Curtis and Amelia gazed in the mirror at their aunt. Esme wondered how to reply to such a sticky question. "Last is a nice man," she said, "but the children and I are a family."

Lily looked at her with sympathy. "Honey, I apologize. It's really none of our business."

"It's all right," Esme said, wanting to settle what appeared to be on everyone's mind. "Actually the children and I still have issues that need to be resolved back in California before we can settle here. I'm certainly planning to return here, but we won't know for sure for a couple more weeks."

"Heard you're going to be the new school-teacher up at the high school," Gretchen said. "The principal was fairly singing over having you on her staff."

"I'm glad." Esme smiled. "I'm keeping my fingers crossed that it all works out. The children are anxious to start school here in the fall."

"No more prying, girls," Lily said. "Can I do your hair for you, Esme? A little treat by way of welcome to Union Junction?"

"I don't know," Esme murmured, tempted and yet uncertain.

"You'll be happy you let her," Violet said. "Lily's pretty good with a wig."

"This is my hair," Esme said.

The ladies laughed.

"They know." Lily got up. "Come with me."

It had been a long time since she'd had time to do her hair or nails. Esme looked with longing at the stylist's chair in the warm and friendly salon, and her heart gave in to temptation. "Thank you. I'd like that."

Once in Lily's chair, Esme was surprised by how her cares seemed to wash away in the bowl as Lily sudsed her. It was such a luxurious feeling!

"Be careful of Last," Lily said with a smile. "The gals have their eyes on the final Jefferson."

"I guessed," Esme said.

"Of course, if he'd been interested, he would have been in here a long time ago," Lily pointed out. "No Jefferson has been shy about going after what he wanted once he saw it."

Esme was too relaxed to worry about jealousy. "I think Last has adventure on his mind more than women." She couldn't even explain how he felt about her. Sometimes she was certain he liked her; other times she felt herself aching as she wondered what was really between them.

The uncertainty wasn't healthy for her or for the children. "I figure it's best if I go my way and plan my family's lives," Esme said. "Truthfully I think Last still has a lot of adventuring left in him."

Lily sat her up, putting a fluffy towel on Esme's head. "It's best not to wait on any man."

"That's what I believe, too. I had several offers for marriage before I came out here, but Last only offered me a home for my children." The truth was a bit painful, but it hadn't failed to escape Esme that since they'd made love in the field Last hadn't come around to see her.

"I heard he applied at the high school, too," Lily said.

"What?" Esme stared at Lily in the mirror.

Lily nodded. "Yes. Mrs. Carrol was in here yesterday crowing about landing Last for a Latin department."

Esme's eyes widened. "That's wonderful!"

"Between the two of you, the high school is really going to be top-notch. We're all very grateful."

Esme didn't want to reveal that everything hinged on whether the judge agreed that Union Junction was the best place for the children. Day and night, she worried about the problem, and her gut always seemed tight with anxiety.

It really wasn't time for her to bring a man into the picture, she thought guiltily, unless she married him.

She and Last had only joked about marriage. It had never been a serious topic.

"So when a Jefferson male decides he wants a woman, does he romance her for a long time?" Esme asked curiously.

Lily laughed. "Not usually. Their courtship tends to be fast and furious and right to the point. Except Mason," she said with a sigh. "He's the type to wear a woman's patience to the bone."

Esme smiled. "I've met Mimi. She's very sweet."

"And likely never going to land her man." Lily shook her head. "Mason is the definition of *elusive*."

"I would have thought that of Last."

"No. Last is just waiting to find the right

woman. He's gotten slower with his romancing ever since he became a single father," Lily said, snipping away at Esme's tresses. "That little baby gets all his time these days."

Esme's heart warmed. "He's been very kind to my kids, too."

Lily nodded. "Last has wanted a big family since he was a child."

"He has a big family!"

"Yes, but…" Lily hesitated. "I think he'd like to do things very differently from how he grew up."

"Oh." Esme nodded. She completely understood. People always longed for the magic of their definition of family.

"Don't worry about it," Lily said suddenly. "Last wouldn't have brought you here if he didn't like you."

Actually that wasn't true. Esme lowered her gaze. Last had "rescued" her, bringing her and the children there because he had a kind heart.

She was determined to show him that she wasn't the kind of woman he had to take care of. Helpless was not her way. "Tell me about these available houses that just need love and affection," she said. "I need to find one as soon as possible."

"I NEED TO GO AWAY as soon as possible," Last told Valentine as he took Annette from her. "I didn't mean to return as soon as I did."

Valentine looked at him with surprise as she put some frosting eyes on bunny-shaped cookies. "Seems you have a reason to stay for a while."

"No," Last said. "I have a reason to leave." He kissed his daughter's cheek. "Would it be helpful to you if I took Annette? If you're in the mood for an extended honeymoon, that is."

Valentine nodded. "Actually Crockett and I still have some combining of our two town houses to do. You know he's knocking down the wall. I'd feel better if I knew Annette wasn't around during construction. I'd planned on asking Delilah and Mimi for help, but if you're available—"

"I am." Last hugged his daughter. "We will go to Lonely Hearts Station for a rodeo and maybe some fishing. Maybe we should drive up to see Uncle Tex and Aunt Cissy and let you float on a raft in the center of a fishpond."

Valentine laughed. "They don't live on a raft or a fishpond."

"Or perhaps we should go sip wine at the Turnberry Estate with Frisco Joe and Annabelle," Last said, letting his daughter play with his hat. "The possibilities are endless."

Valentine looked at him. "What about the possibilities with Esme?"

Last shrugged. "Nonexistent."

Valentine sighed. "Spoken like a true Jefferson bachelor. Down at the church bingo parlor, they're taking bets on you."

"For what?"

"Whether you become a father to three children in less than thirty days," she said slyly.

"Thirty days! Isn't that a bit fast?"

"You always have been. Wasn't Fast Last one of your nicknames?" Valentine lifted her brows.

"I'd have to get married and get a woman pregnant with twins," he said, frowning. "But you're broadly hinting that people think I'm going to marry Esme. Soon."

"Yes."

"No," Last said, "I'm not."

"You sound very certain."

"Of course." He kissed the dandelion softness of his daughter's hair. "Esme understands that I'm cynical and jaded and not the marrying kind. Neither is she. She had plenty of offers right before she came here and turned them all down. What makes the betting boys think I'd have any better luck with her?" he asked. "Nope. Single I'm staying. And I like it that way," he told Annette, who grinned at her daddy.

Valentine frowned. "You don't want to end up like Mason."

Last stopped grinning at his daughter. "What do you mean?"

"Missing the greatest opportunity of your life."

"Why would that be Esme?" he asked. "She is hardwired for independence. Besides, think of the complications of combining two families."

"Jeffersons make all kinds of strange combinations all the time," Valentine pointed out. "It always works out. It's almost like they get better the more combining there is."

Last grinned. "I will not be swayed by your impassioned argument, my lady. The last time someone tried to talk me into marrying, they wanted me to marry you. Think of what a disaster that would have been! You're far better off with my brother Crockett, who, by the way, seems happier than I've ever seen him."

"No, you and I would not have been good marital partners," Valentine agreed, putting the cookies into a refrigerated case. "But then again,

I like a man who appreciates a woman's failings *and* her attributes."

He frowned. "I'm leaving now, as I sense an embedded lecture in that statement."

Valentine stood to look at him. "Could you be leaving behind a woman you're just too stubborn to let yourself care about?"

"No," he said, kissing his daughter's head. "I'm taking Annette with me. Goodbye."

He walked out of the bakery, delighted to get away from Valentine's advice and to have his chubby little girl in his arms. She really was too sweet—he loved doting on her.

Of course, he very much enjoyed Curtis and Amelia, too. Part of his fear about Esme was that he might get real attached to her kids and then she'd pull the rug out from under him. He wouldn't be able to stand that. The reason the town menfolk were betting on his brood enlarging was because everyone knew he loved children and wanted a big family. Wasn't he the one who'd pushed his brothers to increase the number of Jeffersons, starting with Frisco Joe's courtship of Annabelle Turnberry and her sweet little baby?

Once upon a time, Last had heard one of the town busybodies jokingly say that he was the next

Maverick. Eventually, she'd said, Last will be the brother who has his own twelve.

His toes had curled into his boots. Twelve? He didn't have Mason's grit, nor Maverick's joy of life. It was too much, keeping eleven brothers in line. He'd always been the hub in the family's completely bent wheel and he'd felt great responsibility for maintaining their shape. However, now he only had one child and he had no plans for more. He could relax and enjoy the daughter God had given him.

Although Curtis and Amelia would be great kids for any father. Esme was just too tricky for Last. Frankly she scared him.

Valentine tapped on his truck window, so he rolled it down. "You forgot Annette's changing bag," she said, passing it through the window. "And I figured it out. Esme scares you, like Mimi scares Mason. You think you want a sweet Annabelle or Katy, but Last," she said with a grin, "your soul needs more adventure than that."

"Thank you for your wisdom," he said, closing the window as she laughed at him. Disgruntled, he backed up his truck, just in time to see Esme, Curtis and Amelia emerge from the Union Junction salon.

He nearly dropped his teeth. Esme was hotter than a pistol! What had they done to her hair? It was all flowing and shiny, and he could see her face better now. Curtis looked handsome with a little-boy cut, and Amelia swung newly straightened locks with bangs that skimmed her brows. They saw him and waved, and Last cursed the magic that the stylists' scissors had wrought.

Esme didn't need to be any more beautiful. He was already having heart failure as it was. A math teacher asking about her, indeed! And she was just as likely to fall for an academic, studious type as any other.

"Hi," he said, rolling down the window. "Nice. You all look very nice."

Curtis and Amelia smiled, coming over to coo at Annette. Esme hung back a bit, which didn't escape Last's attention. "You sure keep busy," he said.

"There's a lot to do."

He grimaced. "What's next?"

"Lily is taking me to look at some homes."

"Homes?" He could feel his blood begin to boil. "For what?"

"My parents, the kids and I. Maybe a dog."

He had not given her permission to move off his ranch, Last thought. And she hadn't told him she was leaving, as she'd promised to do. Then he quickly squelched those thoughts. Before he could say something he'd regret, he said, "That's good. Annette and I have got to get a move on. We're taking a driving tour, just the two of us."

She smiled. "You're such a good father."

Instead of agreeing, curiosity got the best of him. "So what homes will Lily take you to see?"

"Country farmhouses," Esme said proudly. "She says she has some wonderful candidates."

"Oh?" He tried to stoke some enthusiasm, but it was almost painfully difficult in the face of his desire to keep her near him. Did she have to be such a rolling stone?

"Someplace large enough for my folks. With easy access, so that I can have some wheelchair ramps built. Room for the kids to run. All the necessary things for a family."

Apparently not one thought about him, he realized sourly. "Your parents are moving down?"

She nodded. "It seemed like the best thing to do if we wanted the judge to agree that I was a suitably custodial parent. And remember, they need me, too."

So did he, but he didn't seem to bear any part in this decision process. He felt like an afterthought, and considering the fact that she'd given him her virginity, he was pretty certain he should be one of her regular thoughts.

"So the family plan is that all of you will be in one place. In the wholesome country, in stable Texas. With you teaching instead of lion taming."

She smiled, and he wondered if he'd ever seen such a happy smile on a woman's face.

"I can't thank you enough, Last. This is perfect for my family. Thanks to you, I know that everything is going to work out for us."

He scratched his chin, considering his options. "So I suppose you'll need help moving your parents here?" At least he could be of some service, if only to be close to Esme and the children. Even if she wasn't what she'd claimed to be.

"Oh, I couldn't ask," she said. "You've done too much. My circus friends are bringing my parents down. In fact, the whole circus is coming here."

He blinked. Something like a nervous tic developed beside his hat. "The ringmaster, the lion tamer and the gorilla man?"

"Everyone." She smiled. "They feel that this is an area with great possibilities. According to Delilah Honeycutt—she's a wonderful woman—Lonely Hearts Station could use a stable attraction to add to their monthly rodeo."

His mouth dried out. "Um, that thought had certainly never occurred to me."

"Nor me," Esme said. "It's almost magical how this is all working out. Like I waited all my life for a miracle and then—poof!—it happens like the world's most wonderful fairy tale."

"I guess," he said reluctantly. He couldn't think past the circus idea. Of course, it was brilliant, and trust Delilah to think of it. It would bring so much tourism and revenue to Lonely Hearts Station that it was almost mind-boggling.

It also meant Esme would have very little room for him in her life. Even with that sad thought he managed to say, "Congratulations. It's amazing."

She beamed. "Well, I must go. There's so much to do in the next two weeks."

He felt strangely as if he had nothing of importance to do at all. And yet wasn't this the best thing for both of them? He'd given her assistance, which she'd needed. They'd both stated up front that they didn't want long-term relationships. There was no reason for him to be involved further, except as a friend.

He'd done his duty, Last decided. "I'm glad for you," he said finally. "Good luck."

"It's all because of you," she said softly, leaning

through the window to give him a long, achingly familiar kiss that had him wanting to drag her into the truck to carry her off for an afternoon of burning lovemaking.

The door of the bakery opened, and they both heard it slam. Esme gave him one last peck on the cheek, then hurried off to get her kids. Amelia carefully strapped Annette into her booster seat, then waved goodbye to Last, as did Curtis. They got into their borrowed truck and drove off down the main street of Union Junction, leaving Last pondering what had just happened to him as he remained parked right where he was.

Out of the corner of his eye he saw several interested faces peering around lace curtains at the Union Junction salon. He saw the old men at the church bingo parlor surreptitiously close the front door a fraction more, probably rearranging their bets. On the sidewalk, Delilah and Jerry waved before getting into a truck with Lily, no doubt leaving to take Esme and the kids house hunting.

He felt strangely exposed. His palms itched, but it was nothing like the burn in his jeans. The problem was that this…relationship wasn't as easy as everyone seemed to think it was. Esme was not the type of woman who sat home sedately waiting for the phone to ring. In fact, he wasn't even certain she'd answer.

"If all her good luck is due to me," he told Annette, "I'd sure as hell like some of the perks."

She kicked her feet, but he wasn't certain if she was bored or agreeing. The salon curtains fell back into place; the church door closed all the way. The street was empty of spectators.

"Son of a gun," he muttered. "Part of me is happy she'll be around here forever, even if she wasn't completely honest about who she was. And the other part of me—the rational part—says I'm in Jefferson-size, endless *trouble*."

Surprisingly the latter was a thought he didn't find entirely unpleasant.

Chapter Eight

Mason called to say he wanted Last to eat dinner with him, so instead of leaving town with his daughter, Last headed to the homestead. Olivia asked Annette to eat dinner with her crew—aunt's privilege—so Last succumbed to that, too.

It wasn't until it was just Last and Mason at the long dinner table, void of any personalities save their own, that Last began to realize what life was like for his older brother. Lonely.

There was so much silence in the room that even Helga kept to herself in another room. Mason ate quietly, doggedly, barely looking up. Last wondered why his brother had called him to eat, then knew the answer.

Mason didn't like being alone. For all the marrying and baby-making going on in the Jefferson family, Mason was pretty much going to find himself living at the ranch by himself—if Last left again.

Of all of them, Mason was probably the one who would suffer the most without any companionship. It was a terrible thought, and Last felt sorry for his brother as he sopped up the last of his gravy with a piece of fresh-baked bread. Mason would always have Helga, but that was little comfort, and Mimi had the housekeeper half the week anyway.

No sooner had he thought of Mimi than the silence was broken by the blond hurricane blowing through the front door.

"Hello, fellows," she said, putting Nanette down next to Mason. "Can I join you?"

Helga appeared with two plates as if relieved to have extra company. Mimi grinned at Last. "I've just about talked your brother into running for sheriff. Just because he doesn't want me to run, you know."

"You can't," Mason said.

"I can," Mimi insisted. "But you'd do it better."

"And then what?" Mason demanded.

Last noticed that his brother's entire demeanor perked up now that Mimi was there arguing with him. It was as if blood flowed into his skin and fire lit inside his big body.

"And then I'm going to be a single mother," Mimi said as if Mason were thick—which he was sometimes, Last amended. "I'm going to take care of my daughter and my father."

"Leaving me to do the work in town," Mason said. "I heard there were several still-anonymous candidates who want the job. Neither you nor I need it."

"Mason Jefferson," Mimi said with authority, "you and I make a great team. We could be a great sheriff."

"We?" Mason pushed away his plate. "We? Mimi Cannady, all you've ever brought me is trouble."

"No." She shook her head. "All I've brought you is the only happiness you've ever really known."

Last's eyes widened. Silently he applauded Mimi for spitting the truth right out at his brother. No brother amongst them dared to speak in that manner to Mason. Well, they might, but they also knew they'd be in for a righteous ass-kicking.

Mason sat there quietly, taking whatever Mimi cared to dish out.

"Well," Mason said, "I still don't fancy being a sheriff."

"I fancy the office staying in my family."

"But I'm not your family," Mason said. "So what good does that do?"

"You are my family," Mimi said. "You're just like any other Jefferson brother to me."

Mason stared at her. Last shrugged, looking morosely at his plate, wondering if Helga dared step inside the room to ladle seconds. Then again, if he got up to get the food himself, he wouldn't have to sit and listen to the two of them square off, entertaining though it might be. Nanette threw her milk sippie cup, and both of them reached simultaneously to get it. Mason patiently said, "No, Nanette," and Mimi said, "No, Nanette," and it was like parenting in surround sound.

"I think I'll just mosey off to find Annette," he said, and both Mimi and Mason turned on him.

"No," they said together.

"You be referee," Mimi said.

"I need pie if that's going to happen," Last said, "and Helga's afraid to come in the room."

"Pie, please, Helga," Mason called, and the housekeeper quickly brought delicious pieces of pecan pie that made sitting through the Battle of the Hardheads worth it. Last barely listened to them as they continued discussing the sheriff problem. The good thing, he told himself, was that he and Esme never acted this way. She just ignored him and went about her business, never trying to incorporate him into any plans.

Which was annoying, Last thought with a frown. Wouldn't he rather sit and debate like his brother with his good friend?

He chewed, savoring the sugary pecan flavor, watching the three of them at the end of the table. Nanette made circles with her spilled milk while Mimi and Mason said their piece on both sides. Neither of them listened to the other, and so Last felt no need to referee anything.

In fact, he quietly slid Mason's piece of pie his way, happily forking into it. If only Mimi would come argue with Mason every evening, his brother wouldn't want Last to share meals. Last wouldn't feel guilty about Mason living in this big house alone. Sure, there were plenty of brothers around, but it wasn't the same. When people had new families, they spent all their time with those new families, and single uncles were sort of solitary curiosities.

The debate raged on, so Last reached for Mimi's piece of pie, feeling pretty full but not wanting to pay too much attention to anything that was being said. Nanette looked at him as he snitched the pie, her eyes round with surprise.

"Bad habit," he whispered to her. "Don't start it."

Mimi reached over and pulled her pie back. "Last, this pie is worth its weight in gold. I couldn't allow you to sneak it from me, even though I adore you."

Mason blinked. "You don't adore *me*," he said.

They all sat very still for a moment.

"It was a figure of speech," Mimi said.

"But still," Mason said, "you don't even really like me."

Last looked at the ceiling, wishing he could turn himself into a fly and buzz out the door.

"I like you," Mimi said, "like I like all the boys."

Mason took that in for a second, then looked around for his pie. When he saw that Last had two plates in front of him, he glared at Last. "Last," Mason said, "it's high time you quit thinking everything has to be your way."

Last's eyes bugged. "You have *got* to be kidding me."

"No," Mason said, his tone definitive. "You cannot be the baby with the rose-colored glasses anymore. You have to get a real job and a real life and…you have to stop living off my hard work."

Mimi gasped. Last stared at his older brother, who had suddenly become gargoylelike at the head of the table.

"You've just been on easy street too long,"

Mason said, "and it's time for you to share the burden of running this ranch if you're going to live here."

Mimi looked at Last, her surprise evident. Last shook his head. Mason was just being ornery. Last had always given a fair share of work to the ranch. "It was just a piece of pie, Mason," he said. "Calm down."

"I'll tell you what." Mason speared his fork in Last's direction. "I'll calm down when I've said what I need to say. I've had no less than a half dozen phone calls today wondering when the wedding's going to be."

Last frowned. "What wedding?"

"Between you and that circus-girl magician," Mason said sourly.

"Why would anybody call you?" Last asked.

"I don't know. I thought maybe you could share that information."

"No." Last shook his head. "Esme and I have never even talked about marriage. We've never even talked about dating."

Mason looked as if he didn't believe him.

"She's moving off of the ranch, Mason," Last said. "She's finding a place of her own, and her parents are moving here to live with her." He looked at his brother a bit crabbily. "Not that it's really any of your business, but why didn't you just come right out and ask me instead of going through the charade of having me to dinner?"

Mason shrugged. "Dinner's as good time as any to talk about things. I like dinner-table discussions."

Mimi rose, looking as if she wanted to escape, but Last pointed his fork at her. "Sit," he said. "I sat for yours, now you sit for mine."

She sat and wiped up Nanette's milky mess.

"What exactly is your beef?" Last demanded. "As far as I can tell, you're taking turns chewing on my head and Mimi's. Neither one of us is likely to take it for long. So do you have something else on the brain or can we all get on with some civil conversation?"

Mason wrinkled his brows. "The two of you irritate me is all."

Last and Mimi rolled their eyes at each other, then looked at Mason.

"Mason," Mimi said, "you've got a knot in your tail the size of Texas. And if you don't settle down, I'm gonna give it a jerk you won't forget."

Mason folded his lips in a grimace. "This is serious business," he said. "Last ought to care about his reputation. People are talking."

"My reputation's fine," Last said. "People talk about you, too, but you don't care. Why should I?"

Mason stuck out his chin. "What do they say?"

Last rose to his feet. He took a deep breath. "*They* say that you're a bit of a stubborn mule. *They* say you should have never let me run wild as a March hare. *They* say you should have married Mimi a long time ago, when she was still available." Last glared at his big brother. "But I guess it's too late to worry about what *they* say, don't you think?"

Mimi grabbed up her baby. Mason jumped to his feet. Helga disappeared, the back door slamming. Even the candles flickered on the table before the gale force of Mason's temper.

"Out," Mason said. "Off this ranch right now. Don't let me see hide nor hair of you till a month of Sundays has passed."

"Fine," Last said. He resisted the urge to toss a dinner plate or two as he left. Instead he simply walked out the door.

Mimi looked at Mason, stunned. "Was that necessary?" she asked softly.

Mason stared at her. "If I said it, then it was."

"You picked that fight."

"And I finished it," he said.

"You hurt him," Mimi said. "I saw no call for

that. He's been kind and gentle all his days in this house. If he has lollipop vision, it's because we all liked him that way. Besides, he's grown into a fine man. If anyone has blinders on, Mason, you're as guilty as anyone else."

"Is it true, Mimi?"

She was surprised by his gruff question. "What?"

"That they say I should have married you. That people talk."

She stuck out her chin to match his. "If they do, I don't hear it," she said. "So it doesn't matter."

"It would matter to me."

"Well, it wouldn't matter to me. I'm not living my life right if people aren't talking, Mason," she said, gathering up Nanette and heading to the door. "Personally I think you owe your brother an apology. If I'd been him, I would have pounded you."

Mason looked at her. "I know."

"Damn right." She flung the door shut behind her, holding her daughter to her as she hurried to her truck.

She understood Mason. A big part of her wanted to kiss him because she knew he was in pain and a tiny bit of her wanted to slap sense into his skull. "I never knew such a formidable ox," she told

Nanette as she put the little girl in her booster seat. "But please love him anyway, because he is about to drive off the last brother who has an ounce of pity and compassion for him."

ALL THE LIGHTS WERE OUT in the house where Esme and her children were staying. The bedroom light had just flicked off, and the window was open to let in the breeze.

Last couldn't stand being away from her any longer, especially after his fight with Mason. Too late to call—if she'd even answer. He decided to be more face-to-face. Shinnying up the tree trunk, he thanked his brothers for teaching him the art of drainpipe and tree scaling and tapped on the glass of the raised window.

He heard a muffled scream. Before he could settle himself completely and securely on the branch, a broom poked out the window, attacking him with vigor. Bristles gouged his face and most particularly his mouth. Flailing to save himself, Last lost his balance, falling two stories to the ground to land in a honeysuckle bush, which cushioned his fall, though stabbing him unpleasantly before dumping him to the ground.

"Last!" Esme said on a gasp as she peered down

to see what she'd dislodged from the tree. "Oh, for heaven's sake!"

He groaned piteously, wondering why life had to be so hard for him. It definitely did not seem to be so difficult for his older brethren, and wasn't the baby of the family supposed to have it the easiest? All roads neatly paved for the youngest?

"God, it's a hardscrabble life," he said to himself, appreciatively hearing the front door open with a jerk as Esme came running down the steps.

"Last! Are you all right?"

He moaned for theatrics, but he did feel as if his stomach was lodged somewhere around his head. "You hurt me," he said.

"Well, I should think so! Haven't you ever heard of a doorbell?"

He had, but she smelled so good and the satin of her nightgown was so smooth and soft that he felt his approach had been the correct one. "If I'd rung the doorbell, you would have put on a robe, and that's the best-case scenario. Worst-case scenario is that you might not have opened the door at all. Yet here we are, enjoying a nice moonlit chat on the lawn, just like the old days."

She gently cradled his head, looking closely in the dimness to see if there was blood, he supposed. But it was only his heart that really pained him.

"What old days?" she asked.

"Antebellum, I suppose." He didn't know and cared less, as long as she kept holding him in her lap. "When my mother was alive, we used to have journeys after dark to hunt skeet."

"Skeet?" Esme laughed, and he liked the sound. "Is that a country bird?"

"It's the bird a father conjures when he sneakily wants to teach his sons about the stars and planetary alignment." Last sighed. "Mom would bring watermelon after our hunt—"

"Disguised as an astronomy visual aid, no doubt."

"Don't interrupt," Last said. "I'm trying not to lose consciousness."

"Really?"

She leaned closer to him, and Last felt soft breasts brush his face. The absolute next thing he was going to do, if he ever got the chance to be alone and fully conscious with Esme again, was make certain he enjoyed every single centimeter of her body.

"Do you want me to call Mason?" Esme asked.

"Absolutely not!" The thought was horrifying.

Mason would make the "circus girl" go away—or drive her away, the horrid beast. "I am happy to enjoy the moon with you."

Esme stroked his hair. "Eventually I must go to bed."

"I could lose consciousness in your bed just as easily as out here on the lawn," Last offered.

"I don't think so," Esme said with a laugh. "I think the only bed you should be in may be a hospital bed."

"But then you won't be there," he said, "and I'd probably feel worse than ever." He took a deep breath, ignoring all the various aches and pains in his body. "I had something I wanted to tell you and now I can't remember."

"It had to be important for you to climb a tree," Esme said. "I'm curious. Please remember."

Last sighed. "I can't. But I think it went something like, *Please take me with you in your life.*"

Esme laughed. "That was not what you were going to say. You're trying to get attention. Can you sit up?"

Slowly he eased himself to a sitting position.

"Can you stand?"

Anything to have an excuse to touch her. "You're slippery. But I like the gown."

She put her head under his arm for support. "You seem to be moving well."

"And may I return the compliment," he said chivalrously. "What color is the gown, by the way? It appears to be sort of a muted rose, which is one of my favorite colors."

"Quiet, you," she said. "It's fuchsia."

"Ah, the hot mama of the pinks," he said. "And I feel a deep back on it. *Très* elegant."

"Last!" Esme stopped to look up into his face. "Let me guess—Jefferson men are never too hurt to feel up a woman."

"Not if she's under his arm," Last said happily. "Being hurt and dead are two different things, you know."

Esme gently helped him up the steps. "You could have died if you'd landed on your head. Or been paralyzed."

"Tree climbing is a dangerous art. Discourage your children from learning it."

"If you don't teach it to them, they won't."

"However, I'm not the one who has them trussed and carried to the top of a circus roof," he said, comforting himself that he was nearly inside her front door.

"True," she said, "but they are wearing harnesses.

You had no safety gear. And I don't think you had anything important to say, either." She helped him to the sofa. "Last Jefferson, were you spying?"

"I swear I didn't see a thing. I wasn't even sure if you were in your room," Last said. "I was hoping, of course, but not certain." He relaxed as she covered him with a blanket.

"I'm calling Mason," she said. "You should be examined by someone who knows you."

Last opened both eyes, staring at Esme in the beautiful nightgown. "Esme, I swear you know me far better than my brother ever would. And I really was going to suggest you take me with you wherever you go."

"Like an overly large, overly stuffed bear?"

He shook his head. "Like an overly large, overly big and capable bachelor."

She perched on the coffee table, looking at him. "You wouldn't be happy."

"I swear I would. I have a yen for your magical skills. In fact, you've made the pain disappear," he said, pulling her toward him. "The doctor recommends two kisses and call her in the morning if I don't feel better."

"Her?" Esme said with a smile, though he noticed she didn't pull away.

"She is a superhot doc in Lonely Hearts Station. You'll meet her since you'll be doing circus duty there." He sat back, releasing her. "I suppose you will continue performing?"

She shrugged. "I don't know."

"Mason doesn't like it."

"Why? He rides in rodeos—or did. That's performing."

"But not in fishnets and bikini things that show your luscious curves." Now that Last was thinking it over, he decided only he should be seeing the secret parts of Esme. "It's not exactly beachwear, you know," he grumbled. "Your costume has sequins on it, which draw the eye. Lots of eyes, in fact."

She laughed. "You are such a baby."

"I'm developing an inappropriately possessive streak where you're concerned," Last said. "And Curtis and Amelia, too." He laid his head back on the sofa, thinking about taking a nap. It was all too tiring to sort out at once. A giant yawn escaped him. "Excuse me," he said. "You can just leave me here. Despite that hot nightie, I think I'm too addled to be my usually horny self."

She peered at him. "Maybe you should see a doctor."

"Maybe," he said tiredly, closing his eyes and

wondering if he was going to faint. Then again, if he did, the only place he really wanted to be was there, with Esme and the children. "There are lots of maybes in life," he said philosophically. "Like maybe I should just propose and get it over with."

Chapter Nine

For just an instant Esme stared at the cowboy, his head sprawled back against the sofa. Then she turned him so that he could lie more comfortably. "Propose and get what over with?" she said. "You sound as if you're going to a gunslinger's grave."

He caught her hand, kissing it as if she were a royal princess, before pulling her down to lie against him, spoon-style, on the sofa. "You're just not used to our ways. We Jeffersons like to do things when we've had sense knocked into us."

"Do not try to blame this one on me," she said. "You are accident-prone. I and that curse had nothing to do with it. So keep your proposal to yourself," she said. "And *that,* too."

He shifted so that his erection wasn't prodding her back. "Sorry. Fuchsia's my favorite color."

She rolled her eyes. "You don't see with that part of your body."

"Esme, I think I'm falling for you," Last said, easing up so that he could look into her eyes.

"You fell out of a tree," she said, not wanting to trust him while he was injured and possibly concussed. "You'll be better in the morning."

"But around you I see stars my father never taught me about." Last touched her hair, moving it gently away from her face. "You make me happy. And crazy. Sometimes astonished. Mostly happy."

She smiled at him. "What about Mason?"

"He's a gargoyle," Last said, "though he means well."

"Maybe he knows you better than you know yourself."

"I highly doubt Mason knows any of us as much as he wants to," Last said. "There is a great possibility he has a daughter sitting right underneath his nose and he doesn't even know it."

Esme gasped. "Nanette?"

Last shrugged. "Maybe. Though I used to think he was far too lordly to ever succumb to an affair of the heart. Too busy keeping us all in line to step out of line himself."

"So?" Esme's heart was racing as she thought

about what Mimi was enduring for her love of a Jefferson male.

"So tonight, when we were all at the table, Mimi had seated herself close to Mason, with Nanette at her side. It was the three of them, and then me at the other end, like a saddle sore on a horse's butt. And as I saw them sitting there, a comfortable threesome by candlelight, it came to me that little Nanette looks an awful lot like her uncle Mason."

Esme's eyes widened. "I've never seen the resemblance."

"You wouldn't have been looking, and neither would I. It was only when Nanette tossed her sippie cup that my mind started working. I thought, *Gosh, that child acts like Mason. Stubborn! Hope she's not learning bad habits from her uncle.* And then I realized they had the same nose. That didn't really sound an alarm for me, because noses change as people age. Mine, for example, used to be somewhat smaller and now it's aristocratic."

"Is that what you call the bump in the center?" she asked with a smile. "And perhaps the scar over your left eye is a mark of royalty?"

"All from the bull-riding House of Glory," he said proudly.

"So back to baby makes three," Esme prodded.

Last ran a playful hand along her bare back, so Esme caught that hand in her own. "I like you," he said, and Esme closed her eyes. "We could take a shower together," he suggested, "and you could check me for injuries."

She bit his finger lightly. "No. The story."

He sighed. "It was something Bandera said one day. You know he lives in Mimi's old house with his wife Holly. And one day he was watching Mason carry Nanette across the lawn and he said he wondered why Mason was such a dunce. Now, we've all wondered that many times, so I didn't really pay attention, although Bandera said something about not being able to see that which was under his nose. As I do most of my brothers when they're cryptic, I ignored him." Tentatively he looked at Esme. "I don't know. It was just a strange thought that crossed my mind. I realize the possibility is one in a billion. It would require a certain set of unusual phenomena to line up."

Esme allowed Last to hold her close, his arm around her waist. She had never known this much intimacy with a man. He wasn't really trying to make love to her. It seemed that he was more enjoying talking with her, being with her—while checking out her erogenous zones occasionally—in a sort of "we're friends" way.

She liked it very much. "Phenomena such as?"

"Mason pulling his head out of his butt, for starters. You have to understand, my brother has made a lifestyle out of keeping us on the path of respectability. It takes extreme suspension of belief to think that he might have gone in the very same direction he preached to us to avoid."

"With how much success?" Esme asked doubtfully.

He gave her a light spanking, which went right through her flimsy gown with a delicious *smack!* "As much success as any overly rigid, overbearing brother should have had. Have I ever told you how much I love the feel of your posterior? It's just the right size for my hand."

"Last!" Esme giggled. "I'm more worried about Valentine, to be honest."

"Why?" He bit her neck in the slightest manner, just enough to send chills along her skin.

"I wanted her to like me. You brought me here, and she's the mother of your child."

"Mason really whaled me over getting Valentine pregnant. It didn't matter who she was, it was that it had happened after all his lectures on the use of condoms. If he and Mimi had a child, you can imagine the consequences."

"All the brothers ragging on him forever?"

"That," Last said, positioning himself against her before settling into the cushions with a contented sigh, "and the fact that he could no longer run from himself and his own damnably annoying Code of Behavior."

Esme smiled. "I would think he'd have really needed a rigorous set of rules for eleven wily boys. You obviously got out from underneath his eye enough to learn to climb trees."

"And other things. However, he was not Saint Mason. We knew it, and he didn't want us to." He sighed. "Though I always felt some pity for him, me more than the other brothers. I couldn't imagine being a boy one day and then waking up to find that you were no longer one of the pack but the head of the pack."

"It sort of makes me sad for Mason the boy," Esme said.

"He had Mimi to keep him going, and did she ever." Last smiled, and Esme felt his genuine amusement. "It would be Mimi's best gag if Mason didn't recognize his own daughter."

"I don't think so," Esme said. "I think he'd be heartbroken. Your theory can't be right, Last. Why would she keep it from him?"

"Dunno." Last ran a lingering hand along her bare back. "Did I ever tell you that you're beautiful, like a marble statue only tanner?"

Esme blinked. "For love."

"Yes, my love," he said, snuggling close to her, his erection at her back again.

She flipped over to look at him. "Mimi would keep it from him for love. She would want Mason to love her for herself, not because she had a child by him."

"Oh." Last investigated the ties at the center of her slinky bodice. "Valentine and I didn't get married because we didn't love each other. So I suppose you could be right. Love is very important. Critical, even."

Esme looked up at him, searching for the real Last, the one who didn't like to express his true feelings.

He had a tie undone that revealed some of her skin, which seemed to effectively blow his concentration away from the conversation.

She took the ties, pulling them back together. "You said something about love."

"Did I?" He looked confused. "I think I said that Mimi wants to be loved by Mason."

Esme sighed, realizing she wasn't going to get the answer she wanted to hear. "I think you may have a Mason-revenge thing going on. You're mad at Mason, so you're imagining this whole improbable thing."

"Probably," he said, "but it kept you still for a while." He kissed her neck and ran a hand up under her gown. "You're soft."

"Aunt Esme?" Amelia said, and Esme gasped as Last flung the blanket over her. Fortunately the lights were dim enough that her niece hadn't seen anything, but it had been too close. How quickly Last could make her bend to his sexy will!

"Yes, honey?" Esme said.

"Hi, Mr. Last," Amelia said. "I heard you fall on the ground. I was wondering if you were all right."

"You heard me?"

She nodded. "Curtis and I have a bedroom right beside Aunt Esme's. But we would have heard you howl if we'd been at the back of the house. You were kinda loud."

Esme stood, wrapping a blanket over her shoulders like a shawl. "Last is feeling much better."

He sat up. "Hey, how did you know it was me?"

"Aunt Esme has never had any other man outside her window," Amelia said simply. "And Curtis heard you climbing up. It scared him 'cause he thought you were a bear, so he peeked."

"Oh." Last shook his head. "There are no bears here. At least, none that I've ever seen."

Amelia nodded. "Aunt Esme won't mind if you use the front door."

"Thank you, Amelia," he said, nodding at Curtis, who came to stand beside her, his eyes huge behind his glasses.

Esme looked at Last. "I'm going to put them back to bed. Make yourself comfortable, and we'll see you in the morning."

"No." Last stood, and Esme could see it was an effort. "I woke them up and scared them. I'll put them back to bed."

The children stared at him hopefully.

"I have been told stories by one of the greatest storytellers on Earth," Last told the children proudly. "You may have seen the greatest show on Earth, but your childhoods are not complete until you've heard Maverick the Great's Impressive Lies, Chicanery, Hoodwinks and Outright Untruths."

"Wow," Curtis and Amelia said.

"Can he put us to bed, Aunt Esme?" Amelia asked, her gaze fascinated. "I've never heard a story by Maverick the Great."

"I've never heard Impressive Lies," Curtis said. "I want to hear that one first!"

"Wait until the children share those with the judge," Esme said with a wry smile for her kids. "Yes, you can let Mr. Jefferson put you to bed."

"You sit in the rocker in the room and listen, too," Last told her. "You could learn a thing or two from Maverick the Great. He was quite the magician in his own right."

"Yes, Aunt Esme, sit with us," Amelia said. She looked at Last. "Who was Maverick the Great?"

"My father," Last said proudly. "He believed in education, whether by chicanery or other means— anything to get his twelve boys to pay attention. That makes him great."

"Ah," Curtis said. "We never knew our father."

"Well," Last said thoughtfully, with a glance toward Esme, "I have not seen mine in many years."

"What happened to him?" Amelia asked.

Last shrugged. "That story doesn't end with any more of a conclusion than yours does, unfortunately. I don't know what happened to him. But

I know that wherever he went, he thought about us." He ruffled their hair and pulled off his boots. "Not every story has a satisfactory conclusion, you know, or a happily ever after."

Amelia was silent for a moment. "If you did know, would you be happy?"

"I don't know. I hope so. What I think is that you and me, we're probably a lot alike. We understand that life is not always a fairy tale. But sometimes we get Mary Poppins instead. You have your Aunt Esme to teach you about flying and mixing reality with dreams."

"Who did you have, Mr. Last?" Curtis asked, his voice quavering.

Last wrinkled his lips for a moment. "I was lucky. I had my father, then I had Mason. Sheriff Cannady rode shotgun on me, and old Doc Gonzalez made sure we had all our shots and vitamins and so forth. Nothing can replace the love of a father, I guess," Last said, "but sometimes we have to be happy with what we've got."

"We've got you," Amelia said. "Even if you are telling a whopper about Maverick the Great."

Last grinned. "Oh, no, I'm not. Hang on to your stuffed animals and blankets, kids. I've got a treasure trove of stories just waiting to be told."

ESME FELL ASLEEP in the rocker, and Last fell asleep between the kids, his hat still on his head. In the morning, when Esme awakened, she couldn't help but smile at the family picture they made.

She thought her sister would approve of Last and of him spending time with her children, in spite of the hoodwinks and chicanery issues. She understood he liked to remember his father and that telling stories to her children helped.

Her parents would be moving here very soon, and that would give the children even more adults to look up to. As little stability as they'd had in their lives so far, their new situation was a blessing.

She was very grateful to Last. More than grateful, even. For just an instant, she'd thought he was going to tell her that he loved her.

He hadn't, and her heart felt compressed from disappointment. But as he'd said, not every story ended perfectly and sometimes one simply had to be satisfied with the conclusion.

She didn't want to be like Mimi, never getting her man. The very thought put an ache in her chest. It would be better never to allow herself to fall for the cowboy at all, if she was only going to finish her life's story with a broken heart. She knew there were lots of men on the planet, but that cowboy was special.

She went downstairs to the kitchen, putting a kettle on to boil. His brother wasn't keen on her; she had two children to raise. Last didn't seem to mind the children. In fact, he appeared to want to be around them.

But would he want to do more than spin yarns for her little family?

"Hey," Last said, coming up behind her to pull her against him. "What are you doing up so early?"

"Letting you sleep," she said, her heart beating more quickly. "I imagine you're very sore from your fall."

"Yes. It's not every day I get beat with a broom."

She smiled. "It's not every day a man chooses my window as a means of communication. Telephones are more modern."

"Besides climbing trees," Last said silkily, "I came here last night to ask you some questions."

"Really?" She turned to face him. "You're not just a voyeur?"

"No." Crossing his arms, he leaned against the kitchen counter. "I applied to the high school to teach Latin, since you gave me the bright idea."

"Good," Esme said, "you'll be wonderful. Anyone who can tell such wonderful stories will be a great teacher."

"And speaking of wonderful stories," he said, "while I was applying, Mrs. Carrol happened to mention that you have references from Harvard. Harvard, of all places." He looked at her, and Esme's breath held tight. "Now, why wouldn't I have guessed that a magician would be a Harvard grad?"

She turned away. "If you already know, why do you ask?"

"Because it seems as if you're keeping things from me. And I can't figure out why you wouldn't share that you're highly educated."

"I told you that I was working on a thesis," she said.

"But you never mentioned Harvard. Your omission gives me pause and, frankly, makes me suspicious."

Esme sank into a kitchen chair. "The truth is," she said, taking a deep breath, "after we left England and moved to California, my parents sent me to Harvard to get me away from the circus. Because of my grandparents, who were small-time magicians, it was my dream as a child to be a performer. My parents wanted me to have something more lucrative to fall back on. So I went to college and I graduated and then I came back home. My sister was the one who got married and had kids. The perfect family. Me? Even with the Ivy League degree I…will always love the circus. It's part of who I am."

"Ah," Last said, "even now you're not ready to settle down. And so another audience member is hoodwinked by the sexy and super*sly* Poppy Peabody."

Chapter Ten

"But that was then," Esme said.

Last remained unmoved.

"You offered to help us," she reminded him.

He nodded. Why did her background, her love of disappearing acts make a difference now? Because he'd wanted to believe that he'd swept her off her feet?

She had the broom.

The Curse obviously wasn't working for him. Right now all he felt was betrayed. "I feel deceived," he said, "although I know that may be unreasonable."

"Yes," she said, nodding, "particularly as we both mentioned up front that neither of us wished to be tied down."

"I know," Last said. "I'm confused by my own motives."

Esme looked at him. "Isn't that typical for Jefferson males?"

"I am generally atypical." He crossed his arms. "The problem is that you slept with me, Esme Hastings. You even seduced me. And I liked it."

"So now you want to change the playbook."

He gave her a slanted brow. "I do."

She looked at him. "But you're not in love with me."

"Maybe. Maybe not. You do rattle my cage consistently. I take that as a sign that I should be paying close attention to you."

Esme laughed, turning around to take down two floral teacups. "You are a strange man, Last Jefferson." She poured tea, keeping a wary eye on him. "Though you are a handsome devil."

"That's better." He considered her. "I have decided that I will wait for you to seduce me."

She handed him a teacup. "And if the wait is long?"

He shrugged. "The best things in life are worth waiting for." A frown crossed his face. "Whoever said that didn't have you standing in his kitchen in a frothy nightie."

She blinked. "Part of your appeal is that you really seem to like me."

"Trust me, I do."

"Why should I seduce you, Last?"

"I'm easy." He winked. "I won't make you chase me too hard. But I do think you should pursue. My brothers found their women and—bam!—it was like love hit them upside the head. But I am willing to wait on you."

"I see." She put her teacup down. "I'll think about it."

"I'm going now," he said. "You see I'm leaving."

"Yes, I do," she agreed. "Should you leave from the second-story window?"

"No," he said. "And next time I come by you're going to have to invite me in to see some of that magic your niece and nephew brag about."

She walked close to him, looking up into his eyes. "Here," she said, "this is magic." And she kissed his lips in such a manner that goodbye was nearly impossible.

Yet he had to go if he was ever going to know for sure that she cared enough about having him in her life to come after him.

"Tell me again why The Curse doesn't work for you?" she asked after they'd ended their kiss.

"Because I don't need to be hit by Cupid to know my feelings. I'm not as hardheaded as my brothers."

"Ah." She nodded. "I was becoming concerned. Between the seal and the tree, I worried that you didn't actually have quite the thing for me you thought you did."

"Maybe I don't," he said smoothly. "Guess we'll find out when you pursue. If I turn you down, you'll know."

"What would be the point of my pursuit?" she asked. "If neither of us wants a relationship?"

"Because we could shack up," he said. "If that judge wouldn't complain about you keeping house with a cowboy—"

"He's not going to," Esme said. "He's a friend of my parents."

His throat dried out. "What are you talking about?"

"He wanted to declare my parents the guardians because he knew them so well. He did not know me. My parents have since explained to him that the children are totally happy. They talk to them every night on the phone. They have also explained that they are moving down here and it would be best for the children if I were the legal guardian."

Last stared at her. "So you actually don't need me at all."

Esme slowly shook her head. "Not if helping me keep the children was why you've been hanging around."

He scratched under his hat. "Hell, I don't know why I've been hanging around." He looked at her. "You mean you don't have to go back to California to prove yourself a fit guardian?"

She shook her head in the negative.

"And you've started a new life here and the children are happy and you're happy and everyone's happy but me," he said. "This didn't turn out the way I expected it to."

Her gaze filled with sympathy. "I want you to be happy."

He looked stunned. "I thought you needed me. I wanted to be needed. I liked being the protector for a change."

"I'm sorry," she said. "It's just that everything is different now."

He opened the front door. "Strangely it seems like the closer I try to get to you, the farther away I am." He gave her an intense look that made her want to pursue him, just as he'd suggested. "You'll remember our kisses and you'll come after me."

She watched him silently.

"I'll be going now," he said.

Esme looked at him with her heart in her eyes, but she hoped she hid it from him. "I'll see you soon."

Nodding, he left.

Esme swallowed, her heart hurting...and wanting. She didn't want to say goodbye, but she also didn't want him staying around for heroic reasons. No different from Mimi, she wanted to be loved for herself—not because she was a rescue mission. Last had strong heroic tendencies, as she had witnessed many times. He saw himself in Curtis and Amelia and he related to their circumstance. He would save them any way he could, perhaps even offering to marry her.

But that was no road to happiness.

LAST LEFT ESME'S HOUSE feeling certain that once again he'd been tossed from the bull of life. There was nothing he could do to win this woman—she was keener on remaining single than he was. "And that's saying something," he muttered. "How did she manage to change my mind?"

"Mr. Last!" a small voice called to him. Looking up, he saw Amelia and Curtis waving from the window.

"Hey, sleepyheads!" He grinned up at them.

"I'm going to be Maverick the Great when I grow up," Curtis said.

"No, you're not," Last said. "You'll be Curtis the Awesome. And Amelia the Fabulous."

The kids laughed. "Where are you going?" Curtis asked.

"Hmm." Last considered appropriate answers. "I need to pick up Annette at my brother's."

"We'll come, too."

Before he could say *Probably better not,* they'd disappeared from the window. Seconds later they bounded out the front door.

"Hey," he said, "you didn't tell your aunt you were leaving."

"We have to leave," Amelia said. "She's crying."

"Huh?" Last looked at them with surprise. "She was fine a second ago."

"Yeah." Curtis shrugged. "Sometimes she gets like this. Especially before a big show."

He blinked. "That doesn't sound like the Esme I know."

"She says it's nerves," Amelia offered. "Only she calls them…showtime sillies."

"Wow." Last pushed his hat back. "Are you sure she doesn't mind you leaving?"

"We left her a note on the marker board on the fridge that we were going with you," Curtis said, his round face beaming up at Last. "And since you're only going to Ms. Olivia's, it isn't that far."

Last's mouth twisted. "It's Mr. Calhoun's house, too, you know."

Amelia shook her head. "That's not what Mr. Calhoun says. He says what is hers is hers and what is his is hers."

Last grinned. "My brother is a skilled ringmaster."

The children walked beside him, their little arms swinging importantly as they tried to keep up with his bigger steps, but after a moment he felt two little hands creep into his so that he was in the middle, like tuna fish between slices of brown bread. "You two aren't working me over, are you?" he asked, liking it even if they were but feeling as if he'd better point out that he recognized a railroading when it was happening.

"Sort of," Curtis said. "We like living on the ranch. We were hoping you'd ask Aunt Esme to let us stay here."

"Uh-uh," Last said. "I don't get involved in family machinations. It's a very unhealthy thing to do. The unwise man who steps in the ring usually gets gored."

Curtis pulled a small radio transmitter from his pocket. "Kenny," he said. "Minnie?"

"Yeah?" Kenny's voice could clearly be heard over the walkie-talkie.

"We're here," Curtis said with a grin.

"You little devils," Last said. "Where did you get that thing?"

Amelia skipped beside Last as Curtis ran off. Minnie and Kenny waved from the foot of the windmill that slowly turned as a backdrop to Olivia and Calhoun's home. "Mr. Calhoun says it's the easiest way to get hold of his kids. And his wife, when she's on Gypsy. Today Ms. Olivia says she's going to help us find our seats."

"Seats?" Last was wary. "I still think we should walkie-talkie your aunt Esme. Does she have one of those things, too?"

"No. Kenny borrowed Mr. Calhoun's for Curtis and me."

"Borrowed as in…Mr. Calhoun doesn't know."

Amelia shook her head.

"Let me guess. The four of you stayed up last night radioing."

Amelia gave him a wry look. "Only for a few minutes. Curtis gets tired at night."

"Well, I'll be."

Amelia ran off to join Minnie, leaving Last to walk by himself. He couldn't help laughing, although he knew he was going to be in trouble with Esme. Sighing, he turned around and walked back to her house, this time ringing the doorbell.

She opened the door a second later, her eyes red. "Hi."

"Your kids have made plans by radio with Minnie and Kenny. Something about finding their seats today. I have no idea what all this means. In my day, we just sneaked out. Today's children appear to be more elaborate. All the planning is done by walkie-talkie. But at least there are no broken arms from falling off drainpipes."

Esme smiled. "I knew they were going with Olivia today. She offered to teach them how to ride a horse."

"Finding a seat," Last said. "I get it. I thought they meant a show of some sort."

"Thank you for being concerned."

"I am." He looked at her closely. "The kids said you were having an attack of showtime sillies."

She raised her chin. "It's passed."

Whatever it was, she didn't want to talk about it. "Okay. I'll just be going…again." He stepped off the porch, admiring the fact that she didn't wail about her problems the way some females did.

"Maybe I'll just mosey on up to the main house and see what delicacy Helga is preparing."

"Olivia's also planning to help Annette find her seat," Esme said helpfully. "Valentine bought her her first little cowboy boots. They're pink. Olivia says Annette has just the right spirit for barrel racing."

He stopped in his tracks, then began jogging toward "Olivia's" house, his heart in his throat. When he got there, he saw Olivia turning Annette first one way, then around, then forward, then backward, like a revolving doughnut, in a child's saddle. Olivia was holding her niece carefully. Nearby Valentine watched with a smile on her face. Slowly Last's heart stopped thundering. "Finding a seat" wasn't such a bad thing, he decided, sitting down and wiping the sweat from under his hat. He'd known that all along—even though he'd "found his seat" by trial and error, because he'd been determined not to be left behind by his older siblings.

Along the rail, the four older kids stood watching and patiently waiting for their turn. Out of Kenny's and Curtis's back jeans pockets poked blue walkie-talkies, a matching set. Last sighed, leaning against the fence as he took in his extended family. It could all be so perfect, except that Esme didn't seem to want to be a part of it. And he didn't believe she'd been having showtime sillies for a second.

She was having relationship sillies—a terrifying and crippling panic attack he understood very well.

Chapter Eleven

"Here's a camera," Esme told Last, slipping one into his hand a few moments later and catching him by surprise. "Just in case you'd like a picture of your daughter's first boots and horse lesson."

He looked at her, making her go soft inside. Why did he have to be so fiercely protective of his child, so gorgeous, so smart—and so not right for her?

He took the camera from her, his fingers trembling a bit. "I may not make it through her teen years. You scared me when you told me she was on the back of a horse. I wasn't ready for that."

Esme nodded, looking at the child, who seemed delighted with her ride. "Parenting is the biggest challenge I've ever faced."

"And yet," Last said after snapping a picture and handing her the camera, "you allow your new family to hang from harnesses. I can probably be excused for worrying about my daughter's first riding attempt."

Esme looked at him as she slipped the camera in her pocket. "Last, the children *are* safe. Most importantly, they are with me at all times."

"Yes, but didn't you say your parents wanted you to go away to college so you would give up the circus?"

She nodded.

"And now you're bringing it here, to put on the hootenanny to end all hootenannies," he said. "Which means Amelia and Curtis will be around it all the more. Not that it's a bad thing," Last said slowly, "but when I worry about my daughter's first lesson and you don't worry about high-flying circus antics, I get nervous. See, here I am all worked up about my daughter on a pony. Even if you did decide to pursue me, our differing perspectives make me think I may not be able to live in your world."

Esme shook her head. "They wanted to be part of the circus, Last."

His eyes were deep and brown as he stared down at her. "Anytime my gut tells me firmly something is wrong, I go with it."

She put her hands on her hips. "So we have a different approach to parenting."

"It's something we need to get together on before you start pursuing me," Last said. "So there won't be any misunderstandings."

"There aren't. First, I'm not pursuing you. I thought we established that. Second, Curtis and Amelia like to perform, and as crazy as it may sound, they needed it after their mom died. There's a certain element of suspension of disbelief in the circus, and they really, really needed that."

"Yeah. I know. But it's not the way I think it should be."

Her brows rose. "Maybe it would be best if you worry about your daughter and I worry about my sister's children."

"It can't work out like that," Last said slowly. "We have to agree. What if we become one big happy family living on this ranch…someday."

"Big happy families do not agree on everything."

"But they should," he insisted.

"What family does, Last?" she asked. "Did yours?"

"Oh, hell, no. We disagree from sundown to sunup. But that's not normal."

"Maybe it's very normal," Esme said. "And

maybe I'm not afraid of having my opinion and you having yours and us not meeting in the middle."

"But I really, really think Curtis and Amelia should live like kids. Not circus performers. As well as you turned out," he said, his gaze sweeping over her, "I'd prefer them to enjoy the circus as a spectator sport."

She sighed. "You make a good argument, but I am resisting it."

He looked at her. "Why?"

"Because I'm afraid that if I give in on this issue, you'll feel free to insert your opinion of my parenting skills constantly. I'm aware I'm not the best parent. But I am trying."

"Yeah." He slid his hat back, turning to look at his daughter. "Except for the circus thing, you're doing a great job."

"So are we done having our first major disagreement?" she asked.

He snorted. "That didn't even feel like a disagreement."

"But it had such serious elements."

"Yes. What if we could freely say that was the worst it would ever be between us? If so, we mesh pretty well."

"Well, I wouldn't go that far. I didn't agree to anything, remember."

He turned to look at her, startled. "You did."

"No. I assure you, I did not."

"You agreed that they wouldn't perform."

"Well, in theory. Not all the time is what I meant."

"This is serious," Last said. "It really worries me."

"I know it does," Esme said. "But I think there's something else on your mind. Or you're having an adrenaline rush from running down here."

He took a deep breath. "Parenting styles are important."

She nodded. "I know."

"And from the way you're reacting to my opinion, I don't think you see me in your future," he said.

She looked at him in surprise. "Did you change the subject or is this part of a bigger worry?"

"I'm searching for our compatibility level. Just in case."

"In case of what?"

Last cleared his throat. "In case we decide to be on the same ranch for a while."

"You're not making any sense."

"I know." His gaze went back to his daughter, who was having a great time on Gypsy's back.

"I don't know if I can make sense, not when it comes to us."

"Hey," she said, tugging on his sleeve, "I'm a magician, not a mind reader."

"Yeah." He looked down at her for a moment. "I know. And you're supposed to be pursuing. I told myself not to get too overheated over you, beautiful circus girl."

Waving at Valentine and Olivia and tapping the kids on the top of their heads to say goodbye, he loped off. Esme watched him go, turning to look at Valentine in surprise.

Valentine walked over to join her, an expression of sympathy on her face. "Not that I meant to spy, but I couldn't help witnessing the exit of the Jefferson male."

"Whew," Esme said. "Are they always so abrupt?"

"Well," Valentine said, "I can only speak for my Jefferson male, but an abrupt exit is not always a bad sign. They have their ways, but most of them are good."

Esme appreciated Valentine's attempt to soothe her. "I think your daughter is enjoying her big moment."

"More than her dad did, anyway."

Startled, Esme turned to look at Valentine. "He did take the lesson harder than I thought he would."

Valentine shrugged. "He's a good father." She looked at Esme. "You two seem to have gotten pretty close."

"I'm not sure," Esme said. "But if we did, I hope you'd be okay with it."

"I would," Valentine said. "My daughter likes you."

"She's sweet. And fun. My niece and nephew enjoy her."

Valentine nodded. "They're very good kids."

Esme smiled. "Thank you."

"It's not hard to tell that your sister was a wonderful woman."

Tears sprang to Esme's eyes. She looked at Valentine with appreciation. "I don't think I can fill her shoes."

"And you feel Amelia and Curtis deserve that."

"Yes," Esme said. "But I'm just so different from my sister."

"Different but in a good way," Valentine said softly. "They're lucky you were willing to change your life so much for their sakes."

"Oh, I did in a heartbeat." But Last's words

bothered her. "Do you think it's wrong to let them perform in the circus?"

"I don't know," Valentine said. "Olivia's children performed with her in the rodeo, on the road, even. It was just their way of life. They're fairly well-adjusted. Actually Kenny and Minnie are more positively aligned than some of the adults around here," she said with a laugh.

Esme smiled. "You're making me feel good. But it's not that I want them to perform, really. I just want them to be with me. Last could very well have a point about their need for a slower childhood." She looked at Valentine. "It just seems that we have fundamental differences over how to raise children."

"Because you disagree over performing?"

Esme shook her head. "I had the strangest feeling he was measuring my stepmotherhood ability for Annette." She looked at Valentine. "Not to be indelicate, Valentine. I just mean that it was the strange sort of feeling I got."

Valentine smiled. "It's okay. I'd be worried if he wasn't concerned about a woman he brought into his daughter's life. But you feel he found you lacking."

"Maybe. It seemed that way."

"That would be a problem," Valentine said. "I see why you're worried." She nodded. "The question is, are you worried about your ability to raise your sister's children or your ability to make Last happy?"

"You're never going to believe this," Last said, coming up behind them and startling both women. "Mason just called me on my cell. Mimi's talked him into running for sheriff."

Valentine looked at Esme. "Never a dull moment around here. It's a circus all its own."

Esme nodded, her gaze on Last. She realized Valentine's question had no simple answer, because she was worried about both issues.

Her big problem was the sudden realization hitting her as she stared at the handsome cowboy who had decided he wanted her to pursue him.

She had fallen in love with him—in spite of knowing they were often incompatible. How could two people with so many attached and conflicting family parts mesh successfully?

"It's true," Last said cheerfully. "We are our own big top, complete with clowns." He looked at Esme. "No magician yet, though."

She blinked. "Perhaps a sheriff."

"Well, it would seem so." He grinned. "Mason has to be elected, though, and his opponent is going to be a tough one."

"Who is it?" Valentine asked.

"Me," Last said.

Valentine gasped. Esme stared at him.

"Why?" she asked.

"It will be good for Mason to compete for something rather than just walk into it with his typical sourpuss attitude."

"So you're making the sheriff seat a family matter?" Esme asked.

"Actually I'm making it a personal matter. I want to take a walk on the wild side. Your example inspires me to use my considerable resources in a different fashion than, say, hang gliding."

Valentine smiled, but Esme frowned. "I don't want to inspire you."

"Well, you do," Last said. "I find your dedication to family impressive. I love your commitment to community and your willingness to dig into my issues. Family issues."

"I do not dig," Esme said indignantly. "I just like your family."

"Good," Last said.

"What does Mason say about your decision?" Valentine asked.

"May the best man win," Last replied, "which I was impressed with, until he followed his unusually warm gesture by saying that since only one man was running, he wasn't too worried."

"Uh-oh," Esme said, trying not to laugh. "Well, congratulations."

He grinned. "So you'll vote for me." He really wanted to hear that he had her confidence.

She was silent, still disbelieving of his announcement.

"You did inspire me," he said. "You've set an example of generosity that's making me realize I have to get off my duff."

"When I met you, your duff was already airborne," she said softly. "I'm not sure what you mean."

"I need to quit crying over the past," Last said. "I need to become a major contributor. Before I left for California, registering to run for sheriff was more a whim than anything else, another adventure. But now I know that birth order, unplanned fatherhood—none of that should be holding me back from achieving the best I can be." He tugged on a lock of her dark hair. "I love the way you've faced an awful lot of challenges with a smile on your face."

Valentine cleared her throat. "Congratulations,

Last. You know, I think I'll go help Olivia give the children lunch."

He nodded, but his eyes were on Esme as Valentine walked away. "I didn't say some things earlier that I meant to say."

"You've said a lot," Esme said. "We've moved from parenting issues to family issues, so there's a bunch of material we've covered."

"We Jefferson men are fast," he said, touching her hand. "Try to keep up."

She looked at him. "Truthfully I don't think I can."

His heart pinched, warning him of danger ahead. "Sure you can."

"No," she murmured, pulling her hand away from his. "Magicians know the difference between reality and illusion."

He looked at her, truly worried now. "I go with the flow, Esme. Illusion, reality—I'm used to both."

She shook her head. "No. You're definitely tilting more toward reality, though you may not realize it."

He held her gaze. "You're pulling an emotional disappearing act on me, aren't you? I can almost see the puff of smoke as you disappear."

"Not exactly," Esme said honestly. "But you

think running for sheriff is better for you than the circus is for me. I have enough figuring out to do without worrying about whether you think I fit your version of a good mother."

He raised his brows. "So this gulf I feel between us is really about the children."

"I think so." Esme lowered her gaze. "Though I appreciate you looking out for their best interests."

"Then what's the problem?"

She looked at him, her eyes clear and worried. "The circus is my family," she said.

"Oh." He nodded. "And you feel I've attacked them by not wanting the children to perform."

"Not attacked them, really. It's just that you don't understand them. Or it. They are who I am," Esme said. "Just like you think nothing of running against Mason for sheriff to prove yourself, I look to my family to keep me centered."

He shook his head. "I'm sorry, Esme," he said, pulling her into his arms even as he realized how much he'd hurt her. "Don't disappear over my big mouth. It almost always has a boot in it, but I swear, sometimes it does things you'll love, too."

She tried not to smile as she pulled away. "Last, you're one of the most generous men I've ever met. Not to mention handsome, sexy and smart."

"Well, I'm glad you appreciate my good sides," he said, trying to pull her back to him. "Come back to me and let me show you the good things my mouth can do to yours."

But she remained stiff, and he realized cajoling wasn't going to be the solution. "I need you," he said, "and I can say that because I mean it and I know what my brothers have lost over the years by not speaking their heart soon enough. I have no desire to compete with Mason for the Blindest Heart trophy."

"Just the office of sheriff," Esme said. "You'd be a good one."

"It's great to be the youngest brother," Last said, meaning it for perhaps the first time in his life. "I'm just coming into my own."

"Why?" Esme said.

"I've always been the baby. As the baby, I received preferential treatment and I ruled the roost, a position I was very aware of. I reminded my brothers of their responsibilities and I tried to buffer Mason's hardheadedness with family goals. However, now I can be a role model and a community leader in my own right. I can look outside the family now," he said. "That's something I learned from you."

"I'm not this creature of attributes that you think

I am," Esme said. "However, I did learn the power of laughing in the face of danger—from you."

"Really?" Last scratched his head. "Do I do that?"

"Yes," Esme said with a reluctant laugh. "All the time. It's very attractive in a hardheaded kind of way. Perhaps you're more like Mason in that regard than you think."

"Do I win points with you for it?" Last asked, trying once again to pull her toward him. "Kissing points?" He just knew that if she left now without letting him kiss her, she might not return. Besides, she was acting like a woman who needed a good kiss before she disappeared from his life forever. He could tell he'd upset her—and an upset woman was one who never, ever pursued. The goal was pursuit—he wanted her to want him in her life. "Come here," he said. "I'm laughing in the face of danger."

To his surprise, she melted into his arms. "Not in front of the children," she murmured, "tempting as you might be."

"Sorry about that." But she was so irresistible that he didn't regret wanting her.

She gave him a quick, unsatisfactory peck on the cheek, then left his arms, making him wish they were alone so he could kiss her the way she was meant to be kissed. "Come back soon," he told her.

But as he stared at Esme's retreating back, he realized she'd slipped away from him after all, with no more than a kiss on the cheek for goodbye.

"Drat that woman," he muttered to himself. "I'm going to have to find a different way to show her that we're exactly right for each other, and no circus, family or sheriff seat is going to come between us!"

Chapter Twelve

"Great," Mimi said, coming into the kitchen where Esme was rolling dough with Helga. "Yet another family conundrum."

Esme looked at Mimi, thinking about Last's suspicion about Nanette's father. "I thought that was the family way."

"Yes, but what on earth made Last decide to oppose his brother for sheriff?" Mimi shook her head. "I do not understand him. Mason is like a bear with a sore head now that he's found out his brother is running against him." She lowered her voice. "Secretly I think he's afraid Last might beat him."

Esme rolled the dough flat, wondering how to stay out of this discussion. Mason and Last both running for the same office was a new and awkward position for everyone who knew them. "I have no idea what made Last decide to do that."

"Do you think you could talk to him?" Mimi asked.

Esme hesitated, her fingers stilling as she looked at Mimi. "About what?" she asked, her insides tightening because she already knew the answer.

"Not running," Mimi said bluntly. "I could, but he won't listen to me. You're the one he's listening to these days."

"Oh, no," Esme said, "he doesn't listen to me about anything, I'm sure."

"Well, he told me he got a job at the high school because of you. He said he wanted to be around you all the time so he could keep an eye on you."

Esme blinked. "That doesn't really make me happy. I thought he got the job because he wanted to teach."

"Oh, that, too," Mimi said airily. "But these crazy Jefferson men keep a tight watch on the women they love."

Esme shook her head. "Last does not love me. And even if he did, I'd still be disappointed if he got a job just to keep an eye on me." She wondered if it was true. If so, she was going to talk to him about it.

"I think he was bragging," Mimi said, looking

at the apples on the table before picking up a knife to start peeling them. "I don't think he meant it in a stalkerish kind of way."

"No, I know," Esme said with a sigh. She was beginning to accept Last's craziness. "But anyway, I'm not really in a position to talk to him about anything he chooses to do, Mimi."

Mimi sighed. "It's not going to be good. Jefferson egos pitted against each other has happened before, but this is the eldest against the youngest. Mason is half afraid to beat his brother and half afraid Last will win the election."

"It seems Union Junction is lucky to have two men who want the job," Esme said, trying to change the subject. "How is your dad?"

"He actually thinks it's highly amusing Mason and Last are running against each other. He says he hopes it's a long and vigorous campaign." Mimi grinned. "My father is proud of the job he did and he wants everybody and anybody to run. I was thinking about running for a while, but Mason would be a better choice. He's so steady."

Esme nodded. "But Last is steady, too."

"You know," Mimi said, looking up, "he really does seem to be undergoing a change. I can't quite put my finger on it, but it's a good thing."

"When is the election?" Esme asked.

"Next month," Mimi said.

"How can it be? Don't they have to make signs? Ballots?"

"All that's been done. It's just that none of us knew Last had done it, too."

"How does one keep a secret like that? In California, running for office is a big deal."

Mimi laughed. "This is Union Junction. An election would be more like a handshake compared to what you're used to."

Esme frowned, remembering what he'd said to her yesterday. "So Last signed up to run before he went to California?"

Mimi looked at her. "Well, it would have to have been before, now that I think about it."

"Really. The Last I met in California didn't seem to have any serious aspirations. He never once mentioned a run for office."

"I know. It's so strange," Mimi said. "But I have learned that these brothers do things their way."

Esme shook her head, thinking about the Last she'd met back then, the one who'd tried to help a lost junior sea lion. "He told me he was on a finding mission."

"Well, I know he took Valentine's wedding

hard. I bet that's why he didn't say anything to anyone. And maybe that was even the deciding factor for him," Mimi theorized, stirring some spices into the apples. "The Jefferson men like action and they never get busier than when they feel their lives are going out of control."

"Last wasn't happy when Valentine got married?"

"Well, he was and he wasn't." Mimi smiled at Esme. "You know how that goes. He and Valentine might not have ever had a real relationship, but he adores his daughter, and I think it was hard for him knowing that another man would be her father. Even if it was one of his brothers—as much as he loves Crockett."

"It would be difficult," Esme agreed.

"So it would be just like him to decide at that moment that he needed to show himself and Union Junction that he was still important, too." Mimi shook her head. "Mason is the only one who doesn't really shift into action when he feels threatened."

"Not at all?"

"No," Mimi said, her tone somehow sad. "I think of all the men, Mason is most likely to walk away from anything that made him uncomfortable."

Esme put down the spoon, her heart beating nervously. She couldn't help thinking about Last's theory about Mimi's baby—if he was right, then Mimi had reason to believe Mason might walk away from her forever if he discovered he was a father. That kind of reaction to parental responsibility would be hard to understand, except that Esme's own sister had experienced the same thing. Once he'd realized he didn't want to be tied to a woman—nor be a father—Beryl's husband had simply disappeared.

Mimi had reason to be concerned. Still, it pained Esme. "Mason seems very responsible," she offered.

"Oh, he is. Absolutely. That's why I want him to be sheriff. There's no one better." Mimi sighed. "And one day he'll find the right woman for him and he'll…"

Her voice trailed off, and Esme stood completely still. Even Helga stopped cutting pie dough. They both stared at Mimi.

Then silently Mimi walked out of the room.

Helga and Esme looked at each other, concerned. It was heartbreakingly obvious what secret pretty blond Mimi was keeping to herself—at least to the other women in the room. Mason appeared to be completely blind to the love Mimi had for him.

But Last had known. And he hurt for Mimi. Possibly even for his brother, too.

"Can you finish this?" Esme asked Helga.

Receiving a nod, Esme washed her hands, then left the kitchen.

TEN MINUTES LATER Esme found Last high in the top of a hayloft. "Excuse me," she said.

Last poked his head over the edge. He was sweaty and clearly working hard on something. "Hey."

"What are you doing?" Esme asked, thinking no man had a right to look so wonderful when he was sweaty.

"If you ask, you have to bring cookies and milk with you," Last said. "Come on up."

She wrinkled her nose. "I'm afraid of heights."

He stared down at her in disbelief. "You are not, Poppy Peabody. Illusionists are not afraid of heights."

"I am," she said.

"But you let the kids—"

"I know," she told him. "Would you get over it, please?"

He tossed some pieces of hay down at her.

"I have told you, the children asked to perform. I didn't want to visit my phobia on them, so I let them. They like doing it, and I thought that children who had lost their mother were less harmed by exploring their safety nets than by being blocked from pursuing their dreams."

"You're crazy," he said, "but I like it."

"Last, I can't pursue you," she said.

"Fear of heights?" he said.

"Fear of something," she said, putting her hands on her hips. "But thank you for being so good to Amelia and Curtis."

Sighing, he pulled a kerchief from his pocket, wiping his face and settling his hat on his head. Then he grinned at her. "So spill it. You've been talking to someone in my family."

"What makes you say that?" But she knew his devil-may-care grin was luring her to reveal her heart.

"Time spent in the company of my family invokes a desire on people to babble."

"I am not babbling!" Esme gave him an annoyed glare. "I just thought you should know."

He shrugged. "Okay." Then he went back to work. She could hear a pitchfork thrusting into hay and Last humming under his breath. Taking a deep breath, Esme said, "I think all you Jeffersons must possess genetic code for being supremely irritating."

The whistling continued.

Hands clenched now, Esme eyed the narrow wood ladder that ended at the hayloft. She could climb up there and give the man a piece of her mind or she could stay on the ground and be ignored.

Last peered over the edge again. "I figure if I annoy you long enough, you'll come up here to pester me."

She gasped.

"Most women just cannot stand not to finish giving a man what-for," he said reasonably. "And not even fear of heights will stop them once they get started."

He went back to forking hay. Esme realized her jaw was clenched instead of her hands. How could she ever have imagined that the two of them could be compatible!

"Last," she said.

He looked over. "I could carry you up," he offered.

"No!" That would be far worse! She would faint before they got to the top. "But you could come down here if you really want to have this conversation."

"Not me," Last said. "I do not like conversations where the topic begins 'I can't pursue you.' It just has a bad vibe, you know? Like it's already gone downhill and doesn't have a prayer of the brakes being put on."

He went back to whistling and whatever else he was doing up there, besides teasing her to the point of great agitation. "You are pigheaded, Last," she said to herself, "but you are also right. A ladder is not going to stand in the way of me giving you what-for, you stubborn ass."

With that, she gripped the ladder in suddenly sweaty hands, took a deep breath and scurried upward, only to fall into hands that clutched her securely.

"Oh!" she cried, grateful for Last's strong fingers on her arms. "I will never be able to get down!"

"You will," he said soothingly, kissing her lips, then her temples and then her lips again. He ravished her, making her realize that he hadn't been interested in her phobia at all but merely her body.

"You must stop," she said. "I didn't come all the way up here just to be seduced."

"Sure you did," Last said agreeably, undoing the buttons on her blouse. "And I am damn glad you did."

She felt light-headed and crazily hot. "Let me catch my breath."

"No," he said, giving her a kiss so sweet she

clung to him. "You won't need to catch your breath for what I'm about to do to you. I'll breathe for both of us."

AN HOUR LATER Esme stared up at the skylight overhead, seeing silken cobwebs and maybe a touch of heaven. "I'm not afraid of heights anymore," she said. "I'm positive I like them just fine."

Last leaned up on an elbow to smile down at her and brushed a hand over her breasts. "You never had to be afraid of heights," he said gently. "You could have come up the staircase over there."

Leaning up, she looked to see. Built into the wall was a very sturdy, ordinary set of wide stairs anyone might find in a regular house. "You louse," she said. "Why didn't you tell me?"

"Because you wanted to get over your fears so badly," he said, kissing her neck. "Why else would you come stomping in here all full of pride and glory to tell me you couldn't pursue me—when quite clearly that was exactly what you were doing?"

Gasping, she sat up. "Last Jefferson, I do not like you. You are an egotistical—"

He pushed her back down, straddling her, and

proceeded to ease her skirt up her thighs again. "You're so cute when you're half-dressed."

"You are about to be in big trouble with me," she told him.

He laughed. "So we can have the conversation now that brought you in here in the first place. If you'd like. Which member of my family was filling your head with nonsense?"

She did need to talk to him, but he was making it difficult. Her pride wanted her to flounce out of there, but her body was playing traitor. "Maybe I'll just pursue you as my boy toy," she said.

He grinned. "You would find yourself pursuing often." He nipped lightly at her lips and gave her bottom a squeeze. "You and I are like a matched set when it comes to lovemaking."

"There has to be more than that," she said, "for the sake of compatibility."

"I couldn't agree more," he said, happily admiring a mole on her rib cage. "I have to like you a *lot*."

She sat up, realizing there was no way she could only have a sexual liaison with this too-sexy male. "Sex only goes so far. Can you slide off of me, please?"

He rolled, taking her with him so that now she

sat astride him. "So speak your mind. I'll keep my hands to myself."

She felt oddly more in control in this position. And he seemed sincerely interested in listening. "You're running for sheriff."

"Yes. I told you."

"Mimi says you did all the necessary paperwork before you came to California."

"I did."

"You told me you were on your way to Africa to bungee jump."

"I was," he said. "The two goals are not mutually exclusive. Both required a leap of faith."

"They seem quite different to me."

"On the surface," Last said, tugging her blouse into place helpfully. "However, which would be harder—beating your brother or jumping off a cliff with a harness securing you?"

She was silent.

"You see, you think of harnesses as protection for going up. I see them as protection for coming down. Where's the risk in that?" He tapped a finger against her neckline. "I would say intending to beat your brother for an elected position takes far more guts."

"Why are you doing it?"

He stroked her arm, making her shiver a bit. "Next question."

She took a deep breath. "Mimi wants Mason to win."

"Of course. He's her man, though he doesn't realize it."

Esme felt her heart break a little for Mimi. "I don't understand you men."

"We don't understand ourselves either." Last didn't grin when he said it. "But we muddle through."

"You're right about Mason—"

"Sh," Last said. "Only a blood test could determine that for certain."

True. But she had seen the sadness in Mimi's eyes. "Are you ever going to at least hint to him?"

"No."

Esme took a deep breath. "Because we could be wrong."

"Because it's none of our business and not our life," Last said. "I have enough to do looking after you, lady."

Esme stiffened. "I do not need looking after."

"But I like to." He ran a wandering hand up her back. "So tell me more about this nonpursuit you're conducting."

"Last," Esme said, "why do you think you're immune to your family superstition?"

He grinned. "Because I started that fairy tale. So keep my secret, all right?"

"Fill me in and maybe I will. I may even put this in my thesis about people's beliefs."

"It wasn't magic," Last said.

"But it is a belief system you tapped into, if you're telling the truth," Esme said. "Are you saying that all these years your family has believed in The Curse, you manipulated them?"

"Harsh," he said. "I prefer to think of it as helping them through hoodwinks and chicanery." He ran a hand up her naked thigh, making her glad she'd worn a dress. "Wouldn't that make me a ringmaster who understood his audience?" Last asked with a grin, rolling her over so that he lay on top of her again. "You are now my partner in crime."

"So now what?" she asked him, unzipping his zipper to give him a little of his own medicine. "What about you?"

"Oh, I like having a partner. Never fear."

"About the pain thing."

He nibbled along her neck, then moved to a breast. Her blood soared and sang with pleasure. "I am neither that stupid nor that stubborn. I'd never let my lady go just because I was too stubborn to know a good thing when I saw it."

"I can't believe you've done this to your brothers," she said, gasping, amazed that Last clearly wanted her again as he began removing his jeans. She helped him ease them down eagerly.

"I only do things that are good for them. Trust me, they deserved to be hoodwinked."

She could barely keep her mind on the conversation. The temptation to fall into bliss was too strong. "I clearly remember you being worried about it in California, when the junior sea lion—"

"Shh," Last said. "Let's not talk about that."

She giggled, knowing she'd hit a point of pride with him. "You were so cute thinking you were going to save it. And you distinctly rambled about pain and love."

"A man can come to believe his own legend," Last said. "And something told me I shouldn't take any chances with you. Besides, I prefer to believe in pleasure. Keep doing what you're doing and I'm going to pleasure you again, my lady magician."

She liked having him under her spell. "I could do an entire thesis on you, Last."

But then he took her lips again, and she forgot all about Last's fairy tales.

Chapter Thirteen

Last awakened, looking up at the skylight of the hayloft—if one could call it a true skylight; maybe it was more of a hole in the roof, he decided, and realized he'd never before opened his eyes to marvel at a little piece of heaven. It was all due to the woman next to him, he thought, his heart nearly singing from the joy and wonder of falling in love.

He *was* falling in love, despite Mason's objection to Esme and the myriad other reasons that might stand in his way. Esme was a woman like none other. "You're all mine," he said, confidently rolling over to shower her with affection.

She was gone.

He looked around the hayloft in surprise. "Impatient lass," he muttered. "How kind of her to let me nap while she goes and checks on the kids."

She must have used the hayloft stairs, as he'd explained to her.

But he was worried that she'd just up and leave him napping in hay.

There was probably a very good reason that she'd left his side without a kiss goodbye. She'd been baking apple pies and possibly she'd gone to prepare him a slice, he decided, feeling ravenous after an afternoon of even more ravenous lovemaking.

It was great to be pursued by a gorgeous, good-hearted female.

He headed to the kitchen of the main house, his stomach growling. Helga looked up when he entered, and Mason sat at the table eating a piece of freshly baked pie.

"You look like you've been napping in a hayloft," Mason said, barely disturbing the rise of the fork to his mouth as he spoke.

"Yeah." Not in the mood for a lecture on staying on task, Last said, "Have you seen Esme?"

Mason looked at him strangely. "She and the kids went to Lonely Hearts Station."

Last stared at his older brother, his heart sinking. "For what?"

"You didn't know?" Mason asked. "Apparently her family and the circus are arriving today."

She hadn't said a word, the little minx. Last looked at the pie, almost tasting regret. But there would be more pies in life, yet only one woman he cared about.

"So about the race for sheriff," Mason said.

"First things first," Last said. "I've got to run off and join the circus today, but I'll be back."

"Circus first, then family?" Mason asked.

"Family first or it's forever a circus," Last said, letting Helga hand him a plastic-wrapped piece of pie as he strode out the door.

MOVING VANS were the first thing Last saw when he pulled into Lonely Hearts Station. In all the years of living at the beck and call of glorious rodeo and the excitement it created, he had to admit that the pandemonium surrounding the circus was electrifying.

In fact, he would never have believed it if he wasn't seeing it. And Esme had orchestrated all of this.

For a man used to adventure, his heart was certainly pounding now, with adrenaline, with nerves, with recognition that this was a different bull ride than any he had experienced before. He spied Esme standing with the ringmaster and the lion tamer, directing traffic, and for a moment he watched her in her natural element. Nearby Amelia and Curtis were perched on an empty cage, eating cotton candy. Several Lonely Hearts Salon hairdressers helped unpack, happy to be part of a new venture for their town. The town fathers—including Delilah Honeycutt—stood nearby, smiling at their new economic venture. Esme's parents sat in the shade, looking happy and rested despite the trip. The family was together again.

In spite of himself, Last knew bringing the circus to Lonely Hearts Station was a good idea. Yet his prejudice was hard to get over. He wasn't so different from Mason in that regard; he wanted to believe, as Esme's parents once had, that the circus life was not the most optimal environment for a family.

He was being intellectually dishonest, he knew.

Getting out of the truck, he stood by an elephant that was being taken to the stables, which would be converted for the circus animals. The fact was, the infrastructure of the year-round rodeo was perfect for the small circus, and the commerce would be good for a town that had once struggled so mightily that Delilah had had to lay off half her girls, who had then opened a salon in Union Junction.

He could learn to fork hay for elephants just as

well as livestock. For Esme and the children, he was going to have to change.

"Hey, magician," he said, grabbing Esme and pulling her behind a truck. "Nice disappearing act you performed on me."

"Last!" She looked up at him, her eyes wide.

"Just as soon as I think I've got you tied to me with your fear of heights, you decide you're an air mistress. Maybe I'll get you up in a hang glider one day."

She smiled. "How did you find me?"

He gave her a crooked grin. "You must have said goodbye to Mason. And he has a big mouth."

"Oh." Her eyes glowed as she looked up at him. "He was playing cards with the kids. I had to say something. Besides, it was nice of him to host us for so long."

He kissed her thoroughly, nearly lifting her off her feet, and Esme kissed him back, glad to have him in her arms.

"You weren't in my town that long, lady, and I didn't know Mason knew how to play cards with young children," Last said, pulling away from her lips, to her great disappointment.

"I think they'd roped him into playing Old Maid," she said.

Last grinned. "That is practically Mason's namesake game."

"I think Curtis and Amelia have started to grow on him."

"Believe it or not, he's really not as crusty as he appears. And Curtis and Amelia are cool." He set her down, placing her about a foot away from him. "Back to you just leaving me without so much as a goodbye. I didn't like that."

She lowered her gaze for a moment. "I knew you'd pout about us leaving to do anything with the circus."

"Well, *pout* may be too strong," Last said, knowing full well he'd not given her the support she'd needed with her venture. "However, I might not have been excited about it."

"Whatever," Esme said with a laugh. "Sounds like pout to me."

He twisted his lips. "I'd like to think you'd planned on missing me, Esme."

"Some things about you," she admitted, "and some things not. You're quite stubborn, you know, and I'm not sure where you stand on much of anything. I've realized I need stability." She smiled, and at that moment Curtis and Amelia appeared at Last's elbow.

"There's pie in your truck, Mr. Last," Curtis said, his eyes bright.

"How do you know?" Last asked.

"We checked it out in case you'd brought us some. Mr. Mason called to say you were on your way," Amelia said.

"You knew I was on the way," Last told Esme. "With a pie for your parents. And still you acted surprised."

"Well, I wanted you to feel your trip had been worth it," Esme said. "I didn't know there would be two little pie eaters waiting to see."

"It's all about the pie," Last said with a put-upon sigh. "Here." He handed the kids his keys. "Get the pie, but do not drive the truck, please."

"Yay!" Curtis and Amelia ran off, delighted to be the recipients of truck keys and a pie.

Last narrowed his gaze on Esme. "So I'm not the only one who isn't clear about where you stand," he pointed out. "You knew all along I wasn't going to let you go so easily."

"We work better when you pursue," Esme said, lifting her nose mock-haughtily. "I believe you like the role of hunter."

"I'm going to keep my eye on you," he said. "Right now I'm going to watch you work. I can tell this circus world is going to change my life in im-measurable ways."

She laughed, tugging him by the jeans pocket. "Come help unload and settle my horses. That's where you'll shine, I suspect."

"First, I must say hello to your parents and the ringmaster and the lion tamer and the guy in the gorilla suit," Last said. "I feel like the Wizard of Oz, only I won't be passing out heart, courage and brains."

"That would make me Dorothy."

"You do wear sparkly shoes," Last said, "but I like you naked best. Come on. I'm excited about meeting the gang again."

"HI, MR. AND MRS. HASTINGS," Last said politely as the children dutifully handed them the pie Last had supposedly brought to greet her parents—though Esme knew the gesture was at Mason's behest. Chester lumbered to his feet to greet the cowboy, an old yellow hound glad to reintroduce himself to the once-wounded person with whom he'd shared a sofa. "I see you made the trip just fine, old boy," he told the big dog. "As did the two of you," he said to Esme's parents.

"And you're in much better shape today," her

mother told Last with a twinkle in her eye. "All over your injuries."

"I'm a new man," Last said, not worried about the teasing as he shook her father's hand. "I've been trying to take good care of your daughter."

"So we've heard, dear," Esme's mother said. "The children tell us everything."

He glanced over at Esme, then the children. "I might have suspected," he said, drawing a laugh from everyone.

"Yes, we were a bit worried when we heard that Esme had swept you out of a tree," Mrs. Hastings said, "but it does seem as if you've recovered just fine."

"Oh, those injuries," Last said, and Esme took his arm.

"Let's not tease him too hard," she said. "I'm sure he'll have to adjust to us in small doses."

"I'm good," Last said, stiffening just the slightest when the ringmaster, lion tamer and gorilla-man— today out of costume—came over to say hello.

"We thank you for having us here," the ringmaster said formally. "Being here will keep us all together."

Esme knew that was probably the last thing Last had on his mind. "Mom and Dad and Chester seem to have made the trip very comfortably. Thank you so much."

"It's no problem for family," the ringmaster replied.

Last pushed his hat back on his head, looking at the seven people Esme cared about. There had to be a way for Last to feel included in her life, Esme thought, or he was going to leave her.

She knew then, as he welcomed her ragtag family into town, that she didn't want to lose him. This was going to be a very tough transition for him, because he was used to possessing something completely, and she knew that would include any lady he had a relationship with. He would have to share her, and she hoped he cared about her enough to want to figure out how it all would work.

"We're going to put my horses in their new digs," Esme said hurriedly. "Mom, Dad, I'll be right back to situate you over at Delilah's place."

Taking Last by the hand, she dragged him toward the horse trailer.

"You wanted to speak with me?" he said. "I sense that you have something on your mind, since you've never pulled me away before."

She stopped, looking at him. "Are you going to be okay with all this?"

"Sure." He shrugged. "As long as I don't have to wear a gorilla suit, I'm easy with the whole thing. I really don't like to be confined, and a suit of any kind just isn't me."

She rolled her eyes. "Could we have a moment of seriousness?"

He winked. "We had several moments of seriousness in the hayloft earlier. Is that why you've dragged me into this nice, cool stall?"

"*Last,*" she said firmly, "focus. How would you feel about becoming a father?"

Chapter Fourteen

Last stared at her, his face going ashen. Esme figured that was pretty much her answer.

"You see," she said sadly, "we're probably not going to need you to wear a gorilla suit. You don't have to join the circus or support me in this."

"Wait a minute," Last said, his body tense as he stared at her. "What are we talking about here?"

"I was talking about us."

He blinked. "Of course you were. But did I hear something about becoming a father? Because I already am, of course, a father, and I think—"

"Shh," she said, laying a finger over his lips. "I didn't say I was pregnant. I asked how you would feel about becoming a father. To *my* children." She looked at him, feeling nervous. When he still didn't answer, she finally said, "I am truly not pregnant."

"Oh," Last said. "God, you scared me."

If he'd shot an arrow into her heart, he couldn't have hurt her more. "I didn't mean to. Actually you misheard my question."

"Still." Last put a hand on his chest, then re-arranged his hat. "You totally pulled the trigger before we'd both paced off, magician."

"I guess so." Esme turned around, walking toward the horse trailers.

"Wait." He followed after her, his strides longer than hers. "Can I answer the question, though?"

"You did," Esme said. "And I've always appre-ciated honest answers."

"Yeah, but like you said, I wasn't focusing. I don't have a proper answer to your question, so if you're writing a thesis, the data will be skewed. Flawed. Whatever the proper terminology is."

She felt as if she knew the answer. He liked her. He especially liked her body. He even liked her kids, her parents and her dog. But there were fun-damental differences between them that they could never overcome.

She'd fallen in love with Last, but he wasn't in love with her.

"Hang on a minute, fireball," he said, pulling her toward him. "I love being a father. I've always wanted a big family, just not right now. But I'm more than willing to be dad to your crew. That's the best answer I have, if you're interviewing me for new biological children of your own."

Maybe inside her that's exactly the question she'd been asking more than anything else. Of course it was. She'd been uncomfortable that he didn't see her as mother material to his children—and she wanted a child of her own.

The realization hit her from nowhere and made her lose her breath for an instant. Her heart began burning, like the worst case of heartburn she could imagine. "Oh," she said. "I think I knew your answer already."

"Was it what you were hoping to hear?"

"I don't know what I was hoping to hear," Esme said slowly. "Scientists who compile data are not supposed to prejudice the results."

"I know," he said, his voice full of regret. "You're a work in progress, babe, and everything about you screams *I may be the hottest magician on the planet but I'm also the hottest mom material known to man.*"

"Well, I don't think that's exactly it," Esme said with an embarrassed laugh, "but it's just now hit me that I do want a big family. Bigger than what I have currently. I want to be a mother."

He sighed. "You know, in the beginning we both wanted to be free—"

"I know." She waved a hand to interrupt him so he wouldn't say another painful word. "And there's really nothing worse than someone who won't play by the original rules of the game."

He didn't say anything. Esme wanted to fall through the sawdust on the floor and lose herself in the sifting of dust underneath. He wasn't ready to create a family with her—and that meant he wasn't really ready for sharing a life with her. "I think I'll get on with my job now," she murmured.

"I'll help you," he said, but she turned away.

"I'd rather you didn't," she said. "I'm sure you understand that I just need to…think."

And fall apart by herself.

A moment later she heard his boots moving away from her. When she was certain he was gone, she buried her face in her favorite horse's mane and let the hot tears flow.

LAST FELT LIKE A LOUSE, a new species of louse so low that it was heretofore undiscovered on the planet. Esme had caught him clean off guard, and it had unnerved him for certain.

But in his surprise, he hadn't been very careful with her feelings. The truth was, her question hadn't been that surprising. Everything about her screamed *nurturer, mother.*

To be even more honest with himself, he hadn't really considered becoming a father again. The thought did not usually cross his mind except in the abstract sense that he'd always wanted a big family. But starting that family right now? The thought only seemed to produce a numb response.

He was ashamed of himself. "I have a knack for wanting more than I give back," he said to Bloodthirsty Black, a bounty bull who seemed barely interested in his new animal companions.

Well, there was only one thing to do in the position Last now found himself. Silently he went to help the ringmaster, doing everything he was asked to do. Where muscles were required, he worked. When coaxing was required—such as elephants into makeshift stalls—he coaxed.

And when the newly relocated big top was fairly squared away for the night—and he knew Curtis and Amelia, Chester and the Hastings were tucked away in their beds at Delilah's old place across the street—he got into his truck and headed back to Malfunction Junction, a sadder but wiser cowboy.

FOR THE NEXT TWO WEEKS Esme helped the circus unpack. There was so much to be done! But the more she did, the less she allowed herself to think about Last, and so she determined to stay super-busy. Curtis and Amelia, while missing the ranch, loved being with their grandparents, old friends and beasts both domesticated and non.

Slowly Esme began to realize that she had rushed her feelings. Maybe she had just wanted Last so much in a way she had never felt for anyone that she had let her emotions run too freely. Since she hadn't heard from the hang-gliding cowboy since their last discussion in the barn, she felt pretty safe in assuming that he was feeling as though he'd escaped a noose.

But she didn't regret asking him how he felt about becoming a father. Ever since she had become the mother to Curtis and Amelia, joy of motherhood had begun to blossom inside her.

She had never dreamed she'd want children.

She loved her niece and nephew. She'd loved the idea of being a stepmom to Annette—particularly as Valentine seemed to welcome her. And then fallibility had set in.

She had begun to dream of her own child—many children—with the handsome cowboy.

It was best to know as soon as possible when there was no magic potent enough, no illusion canny enough, to make a dream come true.

"Are you all right?" the ringmaster asked her as she hung her costume in her new dressing room.

"Yes," she said with a wry smile. "Do you think the circus will be happy here?"

"It will be a success," he said confidently. "I trusted your vision. In fact, I find myself liking the woman of the boardinghouse, Marvella."

"Oh, yes." Marvella was Delilah Honeycutt's sister—and Valentine's one-time employer and nemesis and the reason Valentine had first moved to Malfunction Junction. But it seemed Marvella had become a different woman, and it wasn't just that she'd rented out all her old rooms of ill-repute to the circus. She was an honest philanthropist. "I'm happy for you," Esme said with a smile.

"Jerry and Delilah are getting married," the ringmaster said. "I hear the wedding will be in Union Junction. Will you go?"

"No," Esme said. "School starts in the fall, and that's soon enough for me to be there."

"So. A teacher." He nodded. "Good. Still, we will use you here on the weekends and in the summers."

It would be a good source of income. While she hadn't intended to do circus work, Esme realized that just by accepting a dressing room—though she'd always had one with the circus—she had known she would always be a part of this. It was her home, her family, her heart, as she had tried to explain to Last. "I would love to. Thank you."

"Will you marry him?"

"No," Esme said to her friend's abrupt question. "Last and I are compatible on many levels, but not for the final, greatest show on earth."

"Ah, the altar," the ringmaster said with a grin. "Yes, it does require a special sort of magic. And courage."

"Definitely," Esme said, closing the door on her wardrobe. "And we simply do not have it."

He nodded. "Well, you are here, so you will be fine. And Curtis and Amelia are begging me to let them name the new baby elephant, so I must give in to the spoiled condition they developed since living at the ranch."

She laughed. "They did get spoiled at Malfunction Junction."

"Well, it was obviously good for them." The

ringmaster pulled at his long mustache for a moment. "I am sorry, Esme, about the cowboy. I sense you got a bit spoiled, too. It was good for you, as well."

"I did." Esme looked out her small window, cherishing the dark midnight velvet of the Texas sky. "But you know something? The best magic tricks can't make love real if it isn't meant to be, and hoodwinks and chicanery and optical illusions are just special effects to cover what wasn't real to begin with. I'm okay with everything."

She said it, she meant it and she knew it was true. Only her heart disagreed.

Chapter Fifteen

A week later Valentine and Annette found Last in the barn, where he was banging together some sticks and some thick cards that read Last For Sheriff. He couldn't say he minded the company and he was always glad to see his little girl. "Hey, cutie," he told her as she settled into the nest his lap made as he sat on the floor.

"Last," Valentine said, "what are you doing?"

He looked up at her and put on a wry smile. "Hammering."

"Aren't you supposed to have a committee who helps you with such things?" Valentine asked.

"Not many people want to help either me or Mason," he said glumly. "They're afraid to take sides."

"Oh," she said, kneeling down to grab a sign and

a stick and nail them together. "I'm not afraid to take sides."

"Excellent," Last said. "Did you bring me something?" He indicated the large basket she had looped over her arm. "Dinner maybe?"

"No." She squinted at the sign to make certain she'd lined it up correctly. "It's cookies for Delilah and Jerry's wedding. I've shipped over a wedding cake and I'm going over to put it together, but I decided the children would like some cookies." She looked at him. "Are you going to the wedding?"

"Actually I had forgotten it was today," Last said, feeling a little sorry for himself. The truth was, he'd been trying not to think about Lonely Hearts Station—and Esme. He felt like a pariah or an exile, though he knew that was dumb. He was neither, and if he was, he knew why it had happened and there was nothing about it that could be changed. "I guess I should."

"Yes," Valentine said. "For heaven's sake, Last. Put away the pity soup you've been sipping on for the last three weeks and be happy."

He blinked. "Pity soup?"

"Yes," she said impatiently. "You are so not yourself."

"I know," he said equally impatiently, "but I don't know how to be the old me and not be the new me at the same time."

She cocked a brow at him, which could only mean he was going to get an earful. He held up a hand to ward off the lecture he knew was coming. "Look," he said, "I'm fine. Really. The only soup I've been sipping is chicken noodle."

"Usually reserved for people with a problem," she pointed out. "So spit it out."

"The soup?" He frowned.

"The problem."

Of course it had to be the mother of his child who was giving him grief, Last thought crankily. Just about anyone else he could tell to *butt out already*. Sighing, he reached for a cookie out of her basket to comfort himself. "I can tell I'm going to have to have this conversation, because you didn't slap my hand away from the cookies."

She gave him a pointed look. "The faster you start, the sooner we get to Lonely Hearts Station."

"We?"

"Me, you and Annette."

"Where's Crockett?"

"One of many who are helping to put everything together at the rodeo circus," Valentine said. "You are really lost if you don't know that today is the opening day."

Frowning, he wondered how he'd missed all the good info. He hadn't opened a few envelopes on his dresser in the main house, not wanting to do anything but mope. But surely one of his rude brothers could have given him a courtesy nudge.

Valentine looked at him. "Last, let's talk."

He tucked his daughter more comfortably in his lap and looked at the woman with whom he'd created the child he loved more than life itself. "Shoot."

Valentine took a deep breath. "Be happy."

He frowned. "What makes you think I'm not?" Even his conscience refused to admit he wasn't happy. Why should he admit it to anyone else?

"I don't want to overstep my place," Valentine said slowly, "but did something happen to make you not want to see Esme?"

"I really do not want to have this discussion," he said.

She nodded. "I don't, either. Trust me, it's not easy being the one-night stand you forgot about, now trying to convince you that you might be making the biggest mistake in your life by letting another woman go. This is not exactly a conversation I foresaw myself ever having."

He looked at her, appreciating her honesty. "Valentine, I don't think of you as a one-night stand. I think of you as a woman I could have fallen for if I'd been a different man. Subliminally, I knew you were a great girl, and if I've never apologized for my behavior that night, I want to now. You've given me the thing in life that makes me happiest, and for that you will always occupy a place in my heart."

She smiled. "Then you'll appreciate why I want you to have what I now have with Crockett."

His mouth turned down. "I'm not ready yet."

"Of course, it would be best for Annette if both her parents were deliriously happy in life."

He stared at her. "It's not fair to play the Annette card," he said.

"It's just so you'll have to admit I'm right."

"Perhaps," he said sourly, "but she may have to make do with one of us being deliriously happy."

"Well, she could have two happy parents if one of us wasn't determined to ride the range in his stubborn suit and mask of pride," she said, her tone a trifle too sincere for him.

"Valentine, I like my hair suit of stubbornness, my mask of pride and my cloak of bachelorhood," he said. "I don't want to wreck another woman's life."

"Oh. Yeah, I guess not." She stood and put her basket over her arm. He looked at her, perplexed. He had expected her to deny that he'd wrecked her life! And it bothered him that she didn't. "I understand my hair suit," he said. "It's not a gorilla suit or a lion tamer's costume or a ring-master's coat and tails, but it's part of me and I understand it."

"Okay. Have some sugar. You need sweetening." She handed him a freshly baked cookie, and he sighed as he bit into it.

"You have no idea how comforting it is to have a female friend who doesn't argue with me, who doesn't try to make me see another side. I was born not to change my ways and I'm good at it," he said, convincing himself. "I'm so glad you're my friend, Valentine."

"Well, from one *friend* to another, I think you're being rude as hell to Delilah, who did a lot for all of us. I think you're setting a bad example for your child. I think you're being more like Mason than you care to admit and you'll probably lose the best damn thing that ever happened to you. But if you're bent on being a stubborn ass, who am I to wish you were otherwise? I'm no fairy godmother, after all. If you don't want to turn that silly-ass hair suit into a groom's coat and tails, why should I wish you had joy, a beautiful wife and family and a magical happily ever after?"

He stared at her, his jaw dropped so far down that his mouth could have fit his boot toe into it. "Valentine Cakes Jefferson, you swore like a sailor in front of our daughter!"

"And you're being a hardheaded, stubborn dunce in front of her, and I can only pray if she picks up one of our bad habits, it's my momentary lapse. Your way she ends up unhappy—now, tomorrow and for always."

She left the barn, leaving him with his daughter in his lap. "Dang," he told Annette, uncovering her ears, "your mama's got a mouth like a firecracker. Boom, boom, boom! Lighting me up like the sky on the Fourth of July."

Picking up Annette, he walked out after Valentine. "Mouthy women are annoying," he said, "but I'm going to overlook it this time."

She shrugged as she readied Annette's car seat in the truck. "Jerky men are annoying, and I will try to overlook this very unattractive side of you." She looked up at him. "Strong, driven women like Esme do not like men who are indecisive."

He gasped. "Indecisive!"

She faced him, not looking away from his stony gaze. "Indecisive. Equates to being wishy-washy."

"You really like her, don't you?" he said, amazed.

"Last, I've had more worries than I can say about the woman you might eventually bring home to be a stepmother to my child, and believe me, it's not a thought I embrace lightly. But I really, really admire Esme. She has a character most women can only dream of having. She's smart. She's tough. She's strong. And best of all, she loves my daughter. And she loves you." She touched his chin. "You love her, too, and we all knew it the day you pulled up with her in the truck. So why are you throwing it all away?"

"Because I'm a Jefferson, I guess," Last said. What Valentine was saying was beginning to bang a doleful gong inside his head. "You're scaring me."

"I hope so. I hope I'm the ghost of a Jefferson future that makes you want to snatch your life back from the jaws of dissatisfaction and misery."

"Well, I never saw you as a direly warning apparition, but you're definitely giving me goose bumps now," he said. "So are you driving to the church or am I?"

ESME GASPED when Last slid into the church pew beside her.

"Glad you saved me a seat," he said. "I'd forgotten today was the big day."

She stared at him. "The wedding is in your hometown. How could you forget?"

"I don't know," he said. "I think I've been wallowing."

"In what?" Esme asked.

He looked at her and he knew Valentine had been right. Esme was gorgeous. A child sat on either side of her, scrubbed, slicked and beautified to squeaky-clean goodness. She was a thing of beauty in a jade-green dress and straw hat with spring flowers. His breath tightened. What if he had lost her forever? Just because he'd thought he wasn't ready to take the final step to adulthood. "I can't tell you what I've been wallowing in," he said. "Valentine says it's unattractive and nothing to brag about."

"Ew," Curtis said.

"Oh, do share," Amelia said. "It would make Aunt Esme feel better. She said you were probably off on another adventure."

Last shook his head. Not only had he been a jerk

to Esme, but he'd been one to the children, too. A moment of appreciation for the way his brother Crockett treated Annette swept over him. Crockett was a gentleman, a good brother and an awesome stepfather to Last's daughter. "I was not on an adventure," he said. "I was sitting on my ranch missing all three of you."

Esme's eyes widened for an instant, and as the strains of a wedding march began to play and Delilah walked in on Jerry's arm with Mason acting as best man and her sister Marvella acting as maid of honor, Last smiled. "I wouldn't be anywhere but here right now, with the three of you."

"Really?" Amelia asked. "Aunt Esme said you wouldn't be able to come."

Curtis nodded. "She said you'd probably set the pew on fire the instant you sat down. But you didn't."

"No," Amelia said. "Aunt Esme said a church pew at a wedding would probably set Last on fire the instant he sat down, 'cause he couldn't bear to be within two feet of a wedding."

Last stared at Esme. "I feel quite cool, actually."

Esme looked away, her vision trained on Delilah, who was smiling and crying and looking more beautiful than Last had ever seen her. She had that glow about her that Valentine had had on her wedding day. All the other brides of his brothers had glowed with happiness, too. Last swallowed a hard lump in his throat. He must have made a noise akin to a groan, because Curtis and Amelia glanced at him. Giving them an *I'm okay* signal with his fingers and a reassuring smile, he went back to concentrating on the wedding vows.

He'd been so close to getting roped in before and had escaped. However, the woman who had once wanted to stick his head in the marital noose was now advising that he willingly ask the woman next to him and her children to be his family.

More to the point, his new humility in place, he wanted to ask to be part of their family.

Delilah and Jerry said the vows they'd written themselves. Jerry's was a poem of promises he'd composed while on the road, a trucker's ode of joy for the woman he had loved for a long time. Delilah's vows were sweetly spoken words of love and happiness. Last felt himself tearing up, and a tissue was passed down the pew to him from Esme, who was discreetly crying as she watched the couple in front of them.

He didn't need a tissue. He needed Esme and her children.

"I now pronounce you husband and wife," Last

heard, and as the bridal couple turned to walk back up the aisle, applause ringing in the small chapel, he made up his mind.

"Esme," he said, "the only adventure I ever want to be on is the one where I live my life with you."

Chapter Sixteen

Esme stared at the handsome cowboy, her heart beginning a crazy beat. "What kind of adventure are we talking about?"

Everyone had left the sanctuary to throw birdseed on the happy couple, so he was alone with Esme except for Curtis and Amelia. "I've had too much time to think. What that translates into is too much time without you."

She looked at him, realizing that the countless hours—minutes—of missing him had not been in vain. "We missed you," she said softly. "I missed you dreadfully."

Taking her hand, he kissed it. "I'm sorry. I let all the small things confuse me."

Hope bloomed inside her. Could he mean that he loved her? That he wanted that big family of his dreams with her? "I didn't think I'd ever see you again except at the occasional rodeo."

"No," he said, shaking his head. "I called the ringmaster before I came over here, and you'll be seeing me at the circus frequently."

"Oh?"

He nodded. "Yes. He wants to train me as a ringmaster. I've decided not to run for sheriff so that I can devote my full time to you, teaching and being a ringmaster trainee."

Curtis and Amelia clapped their hands and began hopping up and down. Last grinned at them. "Ol' Ringmeister caught me off guard with that one, but he said he needed the security of a substitute every once in a while. He said he knew the rodeo circus was going to be a huge success, but to completely grow into his vision, he needed a partner."

Esme put a hand over her mouth so she wouldn't giggle at the thought of Last in a too-tall hat and formal tails. "Well, I can see you have many attributes that would be just right—"

Last held up a hand. "I know. The ringmaster said a certain amount of blarney was necessary and a great flair for showmanship. Immediately he'd thought of me."

The children grinned, as did Last. "Hey," he

said, "I consider it a compliment if the ringmaster sees potential in me. So I accepted the job." Kissing Esme's hand, he said, "It gave me every excuse to be around you."

She looked at him. "I don't know what to say. What you're saying is more than I ever thought, but—"

"Even a Jefferson man eventually meets his match," Last said with a grin. "And I met mine with you guys."

Curtis and Amelia snuggled up on either side of him, their little arms wrapping around his waist. "So are you going to marry Aunt Esme?" Amelia asked.

"Amelia!" Esme said, laughing.

"I am," Last said, "if she'll have me."

He got down on one knee, ignoring the fact that they suddenly had an audience gathering silently in the back of the church. "Esme Hastings, I love you. I did from the moment I made an unwieldy hang-glider landing at your feet. I could have given up my pride and my stubborn resistance right then and there, but I'll be the most fortunate man around if you'll agree to have me now that I'm a changed man."

Esme began to tremble, and a smile unlike any other she'd ever experienced lit her face.

"Will you marry me, Esme?" he asked. "I promise to take very good care of you and these kids and your parents and Chester and your friends. I need to live in your world and I need to be with you. And about those children you want," he said with a smile, "I can't wait to give you everything you ever dreamed of."

Esme felt tears of happiness pool in her eyes, but she blinked them back and took Last's hand. "Yes," she said. "Yes. Let's live every adventure life has to offer together."

Then she sweetly kissed him, and the moment she did, Last knew he was home for good.

It was the moment he knew he had waited for all his life, and it came complete with a family and a too-tall hat.

Which was, he knew, as the four of them shared a family group hug, a perfect fit.

Epilogue

Esme swallowed a squeal as the harness tightened around her foot, making her bounce back up from the surface of the water. To do this honeymoon bungee jump with Last, she'd had to overcome a lot of fear. But she'd wanted to do it.

It was important for both of them to get over their fears, and he wasn't the only one who'd had a few since they'd met. Almost the second he'd splashed down in the California ocean, she had known this cowboy would change her life.

And he had. For the better.

Bouncing upside down beside her and grabbing her hand was her groom. She looked into his eyes, laughing. "That was incredible!"

"Hearing you say 'I do' before we jumped was

incredible," Last said. "I love you, Esme Hastings Jefferson!"

He was a nut. He was always going to be a nut, Esme knew, but she loved him that way. "I love you, too," she said. "Last, you're going to make an awesome father—a fourth time."

Despite the fact that they were both upside down, she read the joy on his face. "We're pregnant?"

She laughed. "Yes. Just pregnant, so don't freak out. I just skipped, so it's a good thing you didn't want to wait to get married or this honeymoon wouldn't have been possible."

He scowled. "Still. You should be sitting down! You should be—"

"Last," Esme said, laughing, "I love you. But you're going to have to relax. You're way too uptight."

He looked stunned. "Well, that's a first. Everyone always said I needed to be more serious."

Attendants undid their harnesses, trying to guide them to the boat, but Esme began swimming toward the bank, enjoying the feel of freedom. Last followed, grabbing her foot and pulling her toward him. "Hey, bride," he said, "you're proving to be a bigger adventure than I expected."

Wrapping her legs around him, Esme kissed him so that he would completely understand her feelings.

"Wow," Last said.

Esme smiled, completely and joyously in love. It was always going to be "wow" whether under the big top, at a Texas ranch called Malfunction Junction or under this glorious African sky.

She had all the statistics on belief that she needed to know that theirs was a truly happy ending.

*Don't miss the long-awaited conclusion
to Tina Leonard's*
COWBOYS BY THE DOZEN!
It's Mimi and Mason's story in
MASON'S MARRIAGE
(Harlequin American Romance #1117)
Available May 2006!
Turn the page for a sneak preview!

Chapter One

Mimi Cannady took a deep breath as the election results came in. Of course, there had never been any doubt that Mason Jefferson, popular rancher from Malfunction Junction, would be elected sheriff by a landslide.

He came to stand beside her after everyone had finished congratulating him. "Thanks for all your hard work on the campaign, Mimi. Although I'm not sure what new Mimi-jinks you've gotten me into."

She smiled wanly. It wasn't the perfect time to tell him the truth, but she couldn't wait any longer. "Mason, I have to talk to you about something."

"I'm listening," he said. "What does my campaign manager want to tell me now?"

Mimi tried to stop her hands from shaking, but

she couldn't. She willed her heart to be brave and told her spirit that she had faced more difficult challenges.

Friendship was all she'd ever had of Mason Jefferson—and she'd desperately tried to hang on to it over the years.

It was selfish.

They had agreed not to talk about that long-ago night, but now that all his brothers were married and he had a new job as Union Junction sheriff, it was time for her to come clean.

"Mason," she said softly, "Nanette is your daughter."

The victory smile he'd been wearing slowly faded from his face. He stared at her, clearly dumbfounded. "Well, she is, in a way," he said. "I mean, I love her as if she were my very own flesh and blood."

"Mason, the night before I got married—"

"Don't say another word," Mason stated suddenly, his voice cold and hard. He stared at her, a complete stranger she didn't know at all. The longest seconds of his life passed as he studied her face, his gaze hawkish and discerning.

He strode from the campaign war room. Mimi hurried after him, but he turned, holding up a hand so that she wouldn't follow. Helplessly she watched as he got Widow Fancy, who kept the town records, whispering something in her ear.

The two of them walked down the hall of the old courthouse and went into the records room. Where the birth certificates were kept. A loud click echoed in the hallway as Mason locked the door behind them. Realizing what he was about to do, Mimi ran to bang on the door. "Mason! Let me in!"

But there was no reply.

The silence was the worst sound she'd ever heard.

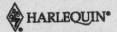

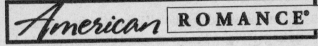

The McCabes of Texas are back!

WATCH FOR SIX NEW BOOKS
BY BESTSELLING AUTHOR

Cathy Gillen Thacker

The McCabes:
Next Generation

Available now:
A TEXAS WEDDING VOW
(#1112) On sale April 2006

SANTA'S TEXAS LULLABY
(#1096) On sale December 2005

THE ULTIMATE TEXAS BACHELOR
(#1080) On sale August 2005

Coming soon:
BLAME IT ON TEXAS
(#1125) On sale August 2006

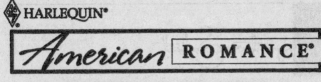

HARLEQUIN®

American ROMANCE®

**IS DELIGHTED TO BRING YOU FOUR NEW
BOOKS IN A MINISERIES BY POPULAR AUTHOR**

Jacqueline Diamond

Downhome Doctors
First-rate doctors
in a town of second chances

A FAMILY AT LAST
On sale April 2006

Karen Lowell and Chris McRay fell in love in high
school, then everything fell apart their senior year
when Chris had to testify against Karen's brother—
his best friend—in a slaying. The fallout for everyone
concerned was deadly. Now Chris, a pediatrician, is
back in Downhome, and asking Karen for her help....

Also look for:
THE POLICE CHIEF'S LADY
On sale December 2005

NINE-MONTH SURPRISE
On sale February 2006

DAD BY DEFAULT
On sale June 2006

Available wherever Harlequin books are sold.

▼ *Silhouette*

SPECIAL EDITION™

PRESENTING A NEW MINISERIES BY

RaeANNE THAYNE:

The Cowboys of Cold Creek

BEGINNING WITH

LIGHT THE STARS

April 2006

Widowed rancher Wade Dalton relied
on his mother's help to raise three small
children—until she eloped with "life coach"
Caroline Montgomery's grifter father! Feeling
guilty, Caroline put her Light the Stars
coaching business on hold to help the angry
cowboy...and soon lit a fire in his heart.

DON'T MISS THESE ADDITIONAL BOOKS IN THE SERIES:

DANCING IN THE MOONLIGHT, May 2006
DALTON'S UNDOING, June 2006

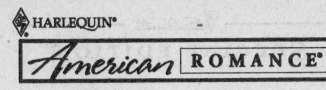

Last grinned. "But don't you feel the magic?"

He was strong-muscled and tall, and the dip in the ocean had left his skin gleaming.

Her nephew and niece looked up at her.

"Do you?" Curtis asked.

"Aunt Poppy?" Amelia said.

Goose pimples rose on Poppy's arms.

"I'm always up for an adventure," Last added with a devilish grin. "And that's what I'm offering you."

Poppy looked into his chocolate-brown eyes. "I don't even know you."

"But it's clear you're in a bind," Last said, "and I've always been partial to coming to the rescue."

"Children, it's time to go. The sun is setting, and that means a bit of a chill this time of year. Goodbye, Mr. Jefferson. And good luck to you on your adventures."

She escaped, her heart pounding. Oh, she *had* felt the magic.

THE JEFFERSON BROTHERS
OF MALFUNCTION JUNCTION

Mason (38), Maverick and Mercy's eldest son—He can't run away from his own heartache or The Family Problem.

Frisco Joe (37)—Fell hard for Annabelle Turnberry and has sweet Emmie to show for it. They live in Texas wine country.

Fannin (36)—Life can't get better than cozying up with Kelly Stone and his darling twins in a ring house in Ireland.

Laredo (35), twin to Tex—Loves Katy Goodnight, North Carolina and being the only brother to do Something Big.

Tex (35), twin to Laredo—Grower of roses and other plants, Tex fell for Cissy Kisserton and decided her waterbound way of life was best.

Calhoun (34)—Loved to paint nude women, and finally found Olivia Spinlove, the one woman who could hold his heart.

Ranger (33), twin to Archer—Fell for Hannah Hotchkiss and will never leave for the open road without her.

Archer (33), twin to Ranger—E-mail and an Aussie stuntwoman named Clove Penmire were this cowboy's undoing.

Crockett (31), twin to Navarro—He was the *first* artist in the family! And his new wife, Valentine Cakes, and her daughter, Annette, have taught him the true meaning of creativity.

Navarro (31), twin to Crockett—Fell for Nina Cakes when he was supposed to be watching her sister, Valentine.

Bandera (27)—With Holly Henshaw in a hot air balloon he doesn't need poetry to keep his mind off his troubles.

Last (26)—The only brother who finds himself a new father with no hope of marrying the mother. Will he ever find the happy ending he always wanted?